HOME

CARA DEE

D1522768

home less

cara dee

mark owners of any wordmarks mentioned in this work of fiction. This story contains scenes of an explicit, erotic nature and is intended for adults, 18+. Characters portrayed in sexual situations are 18 or older.

Edited by Silently Correcting Your Grammar, LLC.
Formatting by Eliza Rae Services.
Proofreading by Rachel Lawrence.

CAMASSIA COVE

Camassia Cove is a town in northern Washington created to be the home of some exciting love stories. Each novel taking place here is a standalone, and they will vary in genre and pairing. What they all have in common is the town in which they live. Some are friends and family. Others are complete strangers. Some have vastly different backgrounds. Some grew up together. It's a small world, and many characters will cross over and pay a visit or two in several books. But, again, each novel stands on its own, and spoilers will be avoided as much as possible.

Home is a novel taking place in Camassia Cove. If you're interested in keeping up with the characters, the town, the timeline, and future novels, check out Camassia Cove's own page at *www.caradeewrites.com.*

DEDICATION

Ketchup hearts
&
Teachers

1

Monday

Slipping between two buildings, I escaped the biting winds and harsh cold to count today's earnings. Hoodie drawn, shoulders tense, ass bruised, jeans dirty, sneakers soaked in snow and at least two fuckers' loads.

My fingers were ice, and they shook as I flipped through the crumpled bills. Mostly fives and tens. Two twenties from BJ, who, not surprisingly, always bought head, hence his nickname. Nasty bastard, but he tipped well.

I needed more.

One more week, and then I'd leave Philly for good. It'd been a fucked-up year. I hurt everywhere, though it did no good to bitch about it.

As I ducked into a diner to warm up and eat my meal for the day, I put my cell phone on the table and stared at it, *willing* someone—anyone—to shoot me a text. My fries and coffee arrived, and I reached for the ketchup. Had Thea been here, she would've widened her eyes expectantly, eager to see how much ketchup I'd use. It was always too much. One might say I ate ketchup with a side of fries. The way I saw it, it was free sugar.

Fuck, I missed her.

Soon. I'd be with her soon. It was the only thought that kept me going most days.

I finished my fries, my stomach nowhere near full, and wrapped my hands around the coffee cup to steal the last of its heat. I didn't have anywhere to go until tonight, so I just sat there. Until my phone fucking finally showed signs of life.

Buck fifty for an hour. Car. Got plates.

I chewed on my lip, considering it. Juan offered quick gigs to free agents, but he was cheap as hell. I texted back.

Two hundred.

He agreed, and I breathed a sigh of relief. I could afford my bus ticket with this.

Later that night, I helped a fucker steal an old car from a dude in South Philly who owed him money. We got rid of the old plates, attached new ones, I got paid, and he drove off.

Tuesday

"Time to head out, guys!"

I groaned and rubbed my face. My head was pounding, and sleeping in a chair—even if I could recline the back—wasn't helping me with my sore ass. When I leaned forward, the faux leather covering squeaked as I grabbed my dirty socks from the radiator and put them on. Billy had been kind enough to stuff my sneakers with newspaper, so they were almost dry when I stuck my feet into them.

Billy stood by the door in his apartment, a place he'd lived in for decades. Walls yellow with cigarette smoke and furniture torn or plain ancient. I didn't know how many homeless teenage boys he'd allowed to crash in his place. What I did know was that he was invaluable to the community. All he demanded from the kids was that they stayed away from drugs. No one was let in if they were high.

He was literally the only man in the world I trusted. I trusted him so much that he had my savings stuffed into an old Styrofoam container in the closet of his bedroom, which was off-limits to everyone who came here. I watched him lock the room whenever I had the chance. It made me breathe easier.

"You all right, kid?" Billy asked me. "I know that chair ain't very comfortable."

I'd gotten in pretty late last night, so the four mattresses in the second bedroom had been occupied by six guys, and the three couches in the front room by another four.

I rose and stretched, my hoodie riding up. My joints popped, something I was too fucking young for. I yawned. "Nah, it was fine. Anything I can help with?"

I wasn't a teenager. The reason he let me crash here most nights—when there was space—was because I helped him out whenever I could by finding clothes and food for those who needed more aid. Many kids who came here hadn't been homeless very long. They knew fuck-all about...most things, really.

"If you come across soap, I'd appreciate it," he said, sparking up a smoke. He let me bum one, since I could never afford my own. "I'd go out myself, but...ya know." He knocked his hip.

I nodded. This winter had been particularly shitty, and the cold made his already painful reminders of being in war more excruciating.

"I'll head out." I pulled out my beanie from the front pocket of my hoodie.

Billy opened the door to his apartment at eight every night, and if I could collect enough money, maybe I could be here then and get my hands on a mattress. It'd been a while.

As always when I got to the door, I tapped the bar sign hanging on the wall that said "Luck of the Irish." Bullshit.

"You should get rid of that, old man."

And his response was fairly predictable. "You'll see one day, Dominic. Even if you're half guido, you'll see. The luck will find you."

I smirked and shook my head, jogging down the stairs of the building. Once I got outside, it felt like tiny ice crystals in the air were trying to rape my lungs.

Wednesday

"I'm next," a beefy motherfucker said.

I turned away from the guy zipping up his pants and wiped my mouth. He threw a twenty at me and left. Music from the bar grew louder for a beat. Then the door was closed again. Three stalls. Me in the middle.

My throat burned.

"How much for a fuck?"

"You got rubbers?" Still on my knees, I squinted up at him. "I'm out."

He chuckled. "Nah, man. What about head?"

"Twenty." I lowered my head, ridden with self-loathing for agreeing. I'd promised myself never to fuck without protection again, but no one fucking cared when it was blow jobs.

Seconds later, I had a monster cock shoved down my throat. My eyes bulged out, and for a moment I considered pulling out my blade and jamming it into his thigh. But I didn't. I needed his money.

He fisted my hair and fondled his balls while he face-fucked me. His wedding ring gleamed.

"You don't look like the queers that," he groaned, "that... usually come here—fuck."

I wasn't queer.

I wasn't anything.

When he hit too deep, I gagged, and my eyes welled up. He gave me a second and jacked his cock fast, spit and come connecting his shaft to my mouth. I drew in a choppy breath, and it was all I got. He choked me again, fucking my throat forcefully until it felt raw and scratched up.

Moments later, his come filled my mouth, and he let out a guttural moan.

I spat it out in the toilet and wiped my face while he chuckled breathlessly and tucked himself into his pants.

He grinned down at me. "Did you say ten?"

I stood up, fists clenched. "Try that, son. I dare you. I've cut a motherfucker for less."

We faced off, and it was my turn to grin. He had no idea. He had no fucking *clue*. I'd been homeless on and off since I was fifteen. I'd defended my sleeping bag with a chain and a crowbar. I'd eaten from Dumpsters. It seemed I was always a heartbeat away from complete madness, and I knew he could see that in my eyes.

The amusement washed away from his face, and he slapped a twenty into my hand before leaving.

On the way to Billy's, I shoplifted three bars of soap from a bodega.

Thursday

Pacing the hallway outside Billy's apartment, I slammed a fist into a wall before screwing my eyes shut and resting my forehead against the door. My aunt's words went on a loop in my head, and I was fucking stuck.

She was asking for more money.

"I wanna be on the bus in three days," I said hoarsely into the phone.

Aunt Chrissy clucked her tongue. "Well, I need money for diapers and all that special food Thea eats. That ain't cheap, boy."

I pinched the bridge of my nose and sank down to the floor. There was nothing I could do. I had to send her the money, but I fucking refused to stay longer in Philly.

"I'll send it." I pulled up my knees and massaged my forehead. "I'll work something out, and I'll be there soon." I inhaled deeply, trying to calm down, and let it out slowly. "You're showing her my picture, right?"

One year. One goddamn year. I'd grown up in cities along the upper East Coast, and when my aunt had announced last year she was moving to some podunk town in northern Washington for a man, I was left with little choice. She was willing to let Thea live with her, but I had to pay for everything, which meant I hadn't been able to move with them. *One fucking year.*

"What picture?" Aunt Chrissy asked.

My heart sank. "My picture. The motherfucking photo of my face that I told you to show her every night." Holy shit, my chest felt tight, like someone was standing on it.

"Oh, that one." She lit up a smoke in the background. "Yeah, I gave it to her. It's around here somewhere."

I gnashed my teeth together and banged the back of my head against the wall in anger and panic. "Does she remember me?"

"I tell her Daddy's coming soon."

"And?" It felt like my last shred of hope rested on her response.

She sighed. "I don't know, Dominic. I'm doin' the best I can here. She's not fucking easy to handle—"

I growled. "*Handle?* I swear..." My hands were tied. Until I was there, I couldn't do shit. I wouldn't be able to do much once I got there either, but at least I'd be able to see Thea every day. "Just...please find the photo. Tell her about me? Tell her I love her." My throat closed up, and I rubbed my eyes. "T-tell her I'm eating a lot of ketchup."

"All right, all right, but I gotta go," she said. "My shift starts soon, and I gotta go down to the ATM to get money for the sitter."

I nodded to myself, then thought of something. I hesitated to ask 'cause I wasn't sure I could handle the answer, but I had to know. "You're bringing Thea wit'chu, right?"

"For God's sake, Dominic, it's just across the square."

"She's three years old!" I shouted. I flew up to my feet and fisted my hair, my gut churning. "I'm *begging* you. Take care of her. It's another week. I'll be on that bus. I have the tickets in my pocket."

I was twenty-four years old, physically fit, and my ticker worked. But I knew what it was like to be dying.

Friday

Last night after ending my call with Aunt Chrissy, I'd stepped out to make more dough. Then it'd been way too late to return to Billy's, so I'd dozed off in a hotel lobby that allowed homeless people to get away from the cold.

Today, I had been out early. As I was already in downtown Philly, I had been close to several customers, and I'd even scored some money selling stolen meat with a buddy.

At eight o'clock sharp, I had knocked on Billy's door. He'd

smiled and tossed me a cutoff chunk of soap and told me to get a shower. The first one in a week. Then...a mattress was all mine.

Four young guys lay beside me, snoring softly. Someone was having a bad dream.

I was dead tired, but my mind was buggin'. I couldn't sleep.

I kept thinking about my daughter. My li'l gangsta. I'd have her in my arms—if she allowed it—in a week. I'd be outta here in two days, sleep on buses as I made my way across the country, and then I'd be with my girl again.

What if she didn't remember me? What if she'd closed in on herself even more and wouldn't even look at me? It was hard enough that she never spoke. I heard her voice so rarely that when I did, I cried.

Aunt Chrissy had said she was touched in the head.

I'd almost cut her. Thea was a fucking genius. She just didn't talk, and she shied away from strangers and panicked at loud noises.

Closing my eyes, I pulled forth memories of her. Her gorgeous face. Those green peepers and an impish grin. She had my dark hair, my smile, and my eyes. She was paler than me and had freckles. Had she changed much? I'd only seen a few pictures, and it had been months.

Reaching into the pocket of my jeans, I carefully held the small photo of her I had. Taped up too many times to count.

Saturday

Billy was helping us forget the outside world tonight. He'd given me cash earlier to buy popcorn and soda, and it was being shared among some ten guys in the living room. I'd bought a can of SpaghettiOs and some bread for myself, but I shared it with a thirteen-year-old boy after seeing the shame and hunger in his eyes. Together, he and I stood in the doorway to the living room as a comedy played on the TV.

"Yo." I broke off another piece of bread for the boy. "Do you have a breakfast spot?"

He frowned up at me, confused, and shook his head.

"Go down to Agnello's around six," I said. "That's when he throws out the bread from the day before." I dipped some bread into the sauce and crammed it into my mouth. "There can be a crowd, and you won't always get any, but..." I shrugged, and then my phone beeped in my pocket.

"Thank you," he mumbled softly.

My forehead creased as I read the text. It was almost midnight.

$150. You know my rules. One hour.

His message made the food in my stomach feel like a rock trying to sink me. Glancing up from my phone, I caught Billy eyeing me from his recliner. He subtly shook his head at me.

He knew only one customer would text me at this hour. Everyone had learned I worked days and early evenings, mostly.

But it was a hundred and fifty bucks. I had my bus ticket, I had change for food on the way, but I'd be stuck in Seattle for a night or two. I'd estimated that was the time it would take me to hustle up what I needed to get up to Camassia Cove where my aunt lived.

Billy walked over to me, his voice low. "Remember last time?"

I nodded and gave the boy the rest of my food. I couldn't eat. "I wouldn't have to do anything in Seattle, though," I said quietly. "I could get on the next bus up north. I'd save at least twenty-four hours."

Billy jerked his chin at the hallway, where we could talk privately. "What about saving your life, kid?"

"That was just one time," I argued, and it was weak as fuck. True, but weak. "He's more into humiliation."

"Last time, he was into putting you in the hospital."

That was a stretch. Billy had taken me to the free clinic to get tested and stitched up. That was all.

"It's my last one," I said. It used to embarrass me that Billy knew I sold sex, but at some point, I'd stopped caring. I couldn't afford it, nor could I afford to say no to this.

So that was how I ended up downtown half an hour later with a cock rammed up my ass.

He wasn't very big, but he fucked like a savage.

The owner of a swanky penthouse, he wanted me to see his wealth. Never his place, but the building was fancy enough. He fucked me in the basement in a nook between the entry to their parking garage and their gym.

He grunted and punched into me harder. "Aren't you honored to be here?"

I hung my head, my hands firmly planted against the wall in front of me. "Yes, sir. I'm very honored."

Die.

I choked on a sharp burst of pain as he reached around me and grabbed my junk. He squeezed it and degraded me for being soft.

"Useless," he spat out. "Don't you realize how lucky you are? Ungrateful little shit!" He tightened his grip, and I stiffened up and groaned in pain.

Die, die, die.

I clenched my jaw so hard I thought I'd crush my molars, and I could've sobbed like a fucking baby when he finally finished and filled the condom.

"F-fuck." I sucked in a breath.

He pulled away and righted his clothes. I knew what was next. Foreplay for his jerk-off session later in the shower.

"Kneel," he told me. "Leave your pants down."

I dropped to my knees and stared at the floor, jeans hanging off my thighs. My dick was limp and hurt almost as much as my balls.

Two fifties landed on the floor. He'd promised another fifty, and there was always only one way of getting it.

I choked up, as if my body was physically unfit to do what he wanted.

"Please, can I have another dollar?"

He snickered. "I suppose." A single landed next to the fifties. I couldn't face him. His light blue eyes were chilling, and while some came off as evil in their manners or behavior, he showed it in his eyes.

To demonstrate his sadistic streak, he dropped the used condom on the money. White fluid seeped out and stained the money I'd pocket soon.

I swallowed against a wave of nausea. "Please, can I have another dollar?"

"You don't deserve it, but I'm a man of my word." He let go of another bill. "Such a shame, really. If you weren't gutter trash, you could've had some potential. Nice body, that thick cock..." He stepped forward and jammed a hand into my hair, fisting it and yanking my head back. "Dago and mick, yes?" He grinned sinisterly. His racial slurs didn't touch me, but that curl of his thin lips did. "Makes for hot men with useless brains." With that, he backhanded me hard and bellowed, "Beg me!"

My head flew to the side, and I gritted my teeth, ashamed and infuriated. My blood was boiling, my eyes stung.

"Please, can I have—" I almost threw up. "C-can I have another dollar?"

It got easier, though. For each time I begged, a part of me died. It usually did. The heat went from a boil to a simmer, and eventually, I ran cold. The only spark that ignited my veins was the knowledge that this was the last time.

Tomorrow, I'd be gone.

Sunday

"Happy now?" I muttered.

Billy nodded sharply, grabbed his cane, and we left the clinic. "As happy as I can be." He stopped me in the parking lot and gave me a brown paper bag. "Mary gave 'em to me. Everyone knows you're leaving."

I peered inside, not too surprised to find a bunch of condoms and clean needles. "You know I don't use." I took the needles out and handed them back. He could give them to one of the kids who were getting hooked out there. "Thanks."

I wanted to say my days of whoring myself out were over, but I couldn't make that promise. Without education and a resume, I would be arriving in Washington with fuck-all to my name and no knowledge of how to score a legal job that would pay well enough.

We took the bus together downtown to the Greyhound station, and I waited for excitement to buzz up inside me. It'd come, no fucking doubt, but I hadn't recovered from last night yet.

"You boning Mary yet?" I asked.

He smacked me upside the head. "Don't'chu talk about her that way, son."

I smiled. They were fucking, probably meeting up during the day. She was always the one who delivered test results, and she went to great lengths, too. Like Billy, that nurse cared for the street kids. She'd tell Billy my results, which I was pretty sure were all negative, and then he'd call me.

"You're never comin' back, are ya?" He cleared his throat, chin held high, and pretended to observe the others on the bus.

"Never." I looked out the window.

There was a ball of emotion stuck in my throat, but I swallowed that shit down. Part of me wanted to hug him and ask him to come with me. That was the loser kid in me who still held out hope that some adults were good people. I'd miss Billy, but this was life.

I owed him, though. Always would. He was the one who stood out.

"If it wasn't for you, I'd be dead." I kept my tone impassive, and it was time to change the topic. "That new cat. The little Puerto Rican kid? I think he'll work." He'd take my place.

Billy nodded. "I think so, too."

"Toughen him up for me," I added. "He shows too much heart—all fuckin' mush."

"Agreed." He paused. "But, don't forget it's about shielding your heart, not killing it. You'll see one day."

I rolled my eyes. How he stayed positive, I'd never know.

We arrived at the coach station as two buses were in the process of being boarded, so there was a lot of bustling about in the waiting hall. I only had a duffel, making it easy to maneuver my way through the crowd.

This was it.

"How many transfers you got?" Billy asked.

"Four." I checked my ticket and compared it to the screen of departures. "Got my first one in Columbus, then Chicago, Minneapolis, and..." I squinted. "I don't know, some no-name shithole in Montana."

In about seventy hours, I'd be in Seattle. Thanks to the money I made last night, I wouldn't have to linger there, either. I'd hop on a bus going north. Or a ferry? They did a lot of ferries out there, if I wasn't mistaken. I'd never left the East Coast, so I was about to learn a thing or two about my own country's geography.

"You got your money?" he asked next.

"Yup." I patted the front of my hoodie.

Last time I got tested a couple months ago, I'd stolen an Ace Bandage from the clinic. Now it was wrapped around my midsection, and I had what was left of my savings tucked into it. It wasn't much anymore, since I'd sent most of it to Aunt Chrissy. Either way, I wasn't setting my bum-ass up to get mugged.

We reached my gate, and it looked like we were right on time. People had started forming a line.

I chanced a glance at Billy, 'cause this really was it.

"I don't got much, kid..." He dug out his wallet, and I was quick to shake my head and gesture for him to put that shit away.

"No way." I kept shaking my head.

He held out two twenties. "You have three days of eating from vending machines. Lemme help. At least get a fucking hot dog or somethin'."

I held my ground and squared my shoulders. "I appreciate it, Billy, but no. You've done enough. And I have a loaf of bread and peanut butter."

It was hitting me now that I'd most likely never see Billy again, and it made my chest feel tight. I needed to keep it light and remember we would talk on the phone, for however long that lasted. I smirked and slapped his shoulder, which was basically all the physical contact I could handle without wanting to cringe or tense up.

"You wanna help, lemme bum a smoke," I said.

He snorted and retrieved his smokes from his pocket. "Have the pack, kid."

There were still fourteen in the pack. It was like Christmas.

I grinned and shoved it into my front pocket. "Thank you." At that moment, they announced the bus to Columbus would start boarding. Those with some pre-check went first, and it made me laugh. "What retarded fuck has priority boarding on buses?"

Billy slanted a lazy grin and scratched his jaw. "Watch your mouth, Dominic." He shook his head. "They're a lot more PC in Washington. You'd be good to remember that."

I rolled my eyes and chuckled. "Oh God, stop." The amusement faded, 'cause there wasn't really much more to say. I blew out a breath, mustering a smile I hoped was convincing. "Thanks for everything, Billy."

He nodded, just a dip of his chin. "Don't be a stranger, ya hear?"

I nodded back and swallowed hard, and then I turned around and clutched my ticket.

Goodbye, Philadelphia.

2

I was a ball of fucking nerves when I stepped off the bus in Seattle. Over the past three days, my eyes had alternated between being closed when I slept fitfully and wide open as I'd taken in the landscapes of my country.

My knees and shoulders popped and cracked as I stood next to the bus and stretched out my arms. I had one more smoke left, so I lit that up and craned my neck to take in my surroundings.

Having never been this far away from home, I half expected to see a vaster difference. But I reckoned bus stations looked the same no matter where you were in the US. With the added fact it was the same people all over who could be found here. Poor folks, backpackers, businessmen in cheap suits—anyone on a tighter budget.

I really didn't wanna spend money unnecessarily, but my stomach was killing me. I'd eaten nothing but bread, chips, peanut butter, and gummy worms. I'd refused to pay for bottled water, and soda was cheaper. What I needed was one meal that settled the hunger and wiped away my headache.

With the smoke dangling between my lips, I left the station

to find a store. It was a new city, people everywhere, and it put me on edge.

Someone bumped into me in his rush to get wherever, and he sneered. "Watch it."

I automatically flinched forward and widened my arms. "Or what, son? You wanna come at me, huh?"

He hadn't expected that, and he settled for a glare before hurrying off and disappearing among the crowd of Seattleites. Seattleans? Fuck if I knew.

I hoisted my duffel higher and ducked into a corner store where I bought a bottle of juice, a yogurt, and two bananas that were on clearance for being a few days too ripe.

After that, I wandered around the neighborhood where the station was and wondered how the hell I'd get to Camassia Cove. I called my aunt to say I'd made it and to ask if she knew how to get there, but she wasn't very helpful.

It was when I was finishing my yogurt that I came to a stop on the sidewalk. Parked on the street outside the bay where all the buses drove in was a pickup truck with a sign on the door that said "Camassia Ink."

I eyed the two guys leaning against the truck. They were chatting while watching a building across the street as if they were waiting for someone to come out of it. Maybe they were.

Assessing them, I didn't think they posed a threat. Possibly the younger guy. He looked to be my age, same lean build, same height, and I reckoned the edge people saw in me, they saw in him, too. Only, he was heavily inked, judging by the tats that peeked out of his shirt along his neck and hands. But they didn't look like gang signs or nothin'. Bomber jacket, skinny jeans, and army boots completed his look.

I hesitated.

The other guy was a nonissue. Aside from the beard, he could be a quarterback who'd missed his calling and become a schoolteacher. A blazer and jeans said it all. I'd been fucked by a few in my day. Either way, he was the safe bet. No edge.

He was the one I'd talk to.

I approached slowly and kept my right hand free in case I needed to defend myself.

"Yo, excuse me," I said.

They turned to look at me. Bomber Jacket cocked a brow and gave me a once-over, and Teach's expression was impassive. No judgment, no skepticism. Good.

"Do you know how I can get to Camassia Cove?" I asked, nodding at the truck. "I'm guessing you're from there."

The guys, who I suspected were related, exchanged a brief look before Teach spoke up.

"Do you live there?"

I lifted one shoulder in a shrug. "I will be, I guess. I have family there—in a place called Camas?"

Bomber Jacket smiled and looked away. "Figures."

I didn't know what that meant, or why Teach shot him an impatient look.

"You can hitch a ride with us," Teach told me, which instantly made me suspicious. "We're just waiting for our brother."

I pressed my lips together. There were red flags. People weren't kind like that for no reason. And I could probably take them on one by one, but *three* brothers? I'd be fucked.

"One day, your bleeding heart's gonna run dry," Bomber Jacket told Teach with a faint grin.

Teach rolled his eyes.

"I don't mind taking the bus," I said.

"Two buses and one ferry," Teach corrected. "Not sure you'll make the last one to Camas, though."

Shit.

The third brother emerged from the office building across the street, and he wasn't surprised when Teach said I'd be going with them. Between a couple jokes and good-natured ribbing, it seemed it was standard behavior for Teach to, as Bomber Jacket phrased it, "take in strays."

I was a stray, I guessed.

I got in the truck and pressed myself as close to the door as possible, knowing I reeked and hadn't showered in days. I couldn't even remember the last time I washed my clothes.

"I'm Adrian, by the way." Teach glanced back at me from the passenger's seat. "Justin." He nodded at Bomber Jacket, who'd taken the wheel. It made sense. He'd taken off his jacket and pushed up his sleeves to reveal arms covered in tattoos. The truck had to belong to him. "And Cash."

That would be the yuppie next to me. He gave me a nod as he got comfortable and loosened his tie.

"Dominic," I said.

I looked out the window to make sure I didn't come off as one who enjoyed chitchat. Fuck that noise. Besides, I didn't like Teach. Or Adrian. His eyes were deceptive. They were kind, some grayish blue color, and I didn't trust kindness.

"Jesus fucking Christ, am I ready to leave Seattle," Cash sighed. "Get me out of this place, Justin."

"I knew you'd be miserable here." Justin eased into traffic and honked the horn at someone who wouldn't let him pass. "Dipshit." After that, it was smooth sailing. "You gonna look at houses?"

"Yeah. I have a week off." Cash nodded, dicking around with his phone. "Did you get your errands done for the shop, or are we stopping somewhere?"

"No, we're done," Justin replied. "Gotta return the truck before seven."

"Surprised you tagged along, Ade," Cash said. "Don't you have kids to bore?"

"Piss off." There was no anger in Adrian's voice, and I wondered if I'd been right. If he was a teacher.

Once we got outta the busiest part of the city, I tuned out the conversation. I saw the Pacific Ocean for the first time in my life, and a breath gusted out of me. It was down to hours. My fingers were literally itching. I couldn't fucking wait to see Thea.

Darkness had fallen when we reached the town called Camassia Cove. I was impressed by the scenery, and I had a feeling it would be even more stunning in daylight. The town was right by the ocean, and driving up here, I'd seen everything from dense forest and mountains to crashing waves and cliffs.

They had some nice digs here. I knew Aunt Chrissy lived in the poorer part of Camassia Cove, but there was no chance in hell it could compare to the ghettos we were used to. Fuck, she'd grown up in the projects in the Bronx.

"Is there a bus stop around here?" I asked, speaking up for the first time in hours. I had Aunt Chrissy's address, of course, but that didn't say much. However, I knew the bus stop that was closest to her, so if I could just get there, I'd find her fast.

"What is it with you and buses, man?" Justin chuckled.

"Public transportation between our districts isn't the best," Adrian explained patiently. "We're in Cedar Valley now. Camas is just north of here, and I'll take you. I live there, too."

I didn't like how that sounded. It implied the other two were heading in another direction.

Shortly after, Justin parked on a cobblestone street lined with old brick buildings that could've been factories at one time. Shops were everywhere, but the sidewalks were empty. I noticed the Camassia Ink sign in one shop window.

"All right, I'm done driving. Don't forget to tip your chauffeur." Justin flashed a smirk over his shoulder to Cash. "I have some work to do, but you know where I live. Lola's got a pullout with your name on it."

"Thanks, punk." Cash inclined his head and opened the door. "Downside of having our folks in Florida now is un-fucking-doubtedly the lack of hospitality. Thank fuck for your girl, Justin."

I got out, too. My breath fogged in the cold.

Adrian frowned. "You know I have a spare room."

"Yeah, in fucking Camas," Cash muttered. "No offense, new guy, but your new home isn't much to brag about. Welcome to Camassia Cove, don't get mugged."

I shrugged. He had no clue.

"You're exaggerating, little brother," Adrian responded dryly. He shook his head and turned to me. "My car's over there." He pointed down the street.

I swallowed and steeled myself. Fuck it, I could take him if it came to that. "Okay." I glanced over at Justin. "Thanks for the ride."

"Anytime."

Then it was just me and Teach, and his car was a rusty one. Not a truck, which were everywhere in this fucking state. Someone had spray-painted on the side of the door. Shitty orange graffiti on metallic blue.

I sat down in the back, creating some distance between us, and I ignored his strange look.

Next to me were a handful of textbooks about history.

"Are you a teacher?" I asked.

"I am."

I nodded. Knew it.

He pulled away from the curb, and I tapped my leg impatiently. I was nervous as fuck. And scared shitless Thea had forgotten me, but I didn't wanna think about it.

"I teach history at Camas High." He flicked his gaze at me in the rearview mirror. "I meant what I told my brother. Camas isn't that bad, especially if—judging by your accent—you're from...New York?"

"All over that area." I scratched my filthy hair through the beanie and looked out the window. A shower would be awesome. Dirt itched. "Philly most recently."

Soon, the houses were gone, as was the cozy cobblestone crap and the shops. I tensed up as we drove deeper into a forest. It was pitch black, but it didn't last more than a few minutes.

I exhaled. I saw buildings again.

They didn't look bad at all. A bit run-down, maybe. Same kinda buildings that were all over Brooklyn, Harlem, and Queens—just not as high. Most of them were three or four stories. The streets had more potholes. Shops had barred windows, and it looked like Camas was the home of fucking awful graffiti.

"What's the address?"

Should I tell him? No. Fuck that. "Um, the bus stop is called Olympia Square."

"Fair enough. It's close to where I live." He slowed down at an intersection, and I looked around. Some streetlights were broken. One corner store was open, and a few kids were hanging outside. "If you're planning on taking said bus often, I can tell you it stops running after ten on weekends, eleven on weeknights. And the one bus that goes through the Valley and Camas to Downtown is always half an hour late. Most people drive here."

"Got it." My knee bounced. I was mere minutes away from seeing my daughter for the first time in a year. "I don't got a license, so..." I shrugged.

I hoped it wouldn't be too difficult to make money. Worst-case scenario, I'd have to return to Seattle. Make dough there, then travel up here as often as possible. But first, I wanted to see what options I had, and as much as I hated selling my ass, it was a place to start.

The knot in my stomach grew and grew. I hadn't been this nervous since Thea was born. I saw the tiny-as-fuck square; it was right up ahead, and Teach was telling me about the four streets that connected here. One of them was the one Aunt Chrissy lived on, so that was good.

"Are you okay, Dominic?"

I nodded but didn't speak.

Adrian pulled over, and I opened the door a few inches in case he got any ideas. An escape route was always good to have.

"Thank you for everything," I said. "Oh, um—are there any gay bars around here?"

Adrian's brows flew up. "Ah..." He cleared his throat. "There are a couple down in the Valley. None here..." He looked away and drummed his fingers along the wheel. I could tell he had more info on that. "Kings Park, down that street. There's some... activity, if you will."

I grinned. "You mean cruising."

His smile was stiff, and I could bet the look in his eyes was usually reserved for a student who was pushing his luck.

"Yes. Cruising."

"Aight." I got outta the car and tapped the roof. "Thanks again, Teach."

I closed the door, and then I waited for him to pull away from the curb before I made my way across the empty square.

Concrete seats and tables made me guess old fuckers played chess in the shade of the trees in the summer.

It was as cold here as it was in Philly, but the winds weren't as harsh. The air wasn't as sharp. Almost like the sea softened it...? Whatever. It was still frigid, and I didn't have a jacket.

I reached St. Claire Avenue, and before I knew it, I was standing before Aunt Chrissy's building.

My feet were stuck. Our last name was right there, next to the button I'd push so she could buzz me in.

Rubbing my hands together, I blew out a breath in between them to warm 'em up. The three-story building would look pathetic among the skyscrapers where I grew up, yet it seemed terrifying right now.

What if she'd forgotten me?

I'd had such visions before we parted. I'd call every night and make sure she heard my voice.

Bad call—literally. Her sobbing and screaming had torn me the fuck apart. So, I'd gone down to a couple calls a week. She got fussy. Once a week. Utterly confused and uninterested.

Last time was her birthday, right before Thanksgiving. She hadn't made a sound. Now a new year had started.

Staring at the ground, I clenched my jaw and pulled myself together. One step. Another step. I lifted my arm, and I pushed the damn button next to "Cleary."

The intercom crackled, but I heard my aunt's voice, and I managed to croak out it was me.

"'Bout time, kid."

She buzzed me in, and I forced my legs to carry me to the second floor. Removing my beanie, I ran a shaky hand through my hair and grimaced. Thea shouldn't see me this way. The devil would be scared.

I knocked on the door, and my aunt opened it. A short,

stacked woman with bitterness and alcoholism etched on her face. Addiction ran in the family, most on my dad's side.

"I got it under control," Dad would say defensively. "I'm Irish."

Liver disease liked the Irish too, though.

"Good to see ya." Aunt Chrissy smiled up at me and wrinkled her nose. "You look like shit—like your dad, rest his soul."

Rest his soul? Fuck that deadbeat bitch.

"Is-is she awake?" I asked nervously.

She nodded. "You might wanna shower first, though."

She was right. I didn't wanna waste another fucking minute being away from her, but I couldn't look like this. Or smell like this.

"Thank you." I dumped my bag on the floor and hesitated in the hallway. It wasn't a big apartment, so I could see the kitchen, the entrance to the living room, and a hallway that presumably led to a bedroom or two.

"Go on, get!" Aunt Chrissy shooed me. "I'll find somethin' of Glenn's you can wear."

I was half surprised she'd kept her man around this long.

"Aight, thanks." I disappeared down the hall, noticing the living room was empty, and into the bathroom that was open.

Fifteen minutes later, I'd showered, shaved, and brushed my teeth. A pair of sweats and a T-shirt waited for me on the counter, so I put them on and shivered. It was cold. Dirty skin actually provided protection from the weather. Now I felt fucking naked.

"Thea!" my aunt hollered. "Come see your father!"

I stopped dead in my tracks as a tiny girl with dark hair ran past me in the narrow hallway.

I blinked. It was like time slowed down, and I didn't remember walking to the living room. I didn't remember ending up there at all. I only saw this li'l slip of a person with curls that bounced when she ran, a baby-pink tee, and a butt covered in a diaper. She needed some meat on her bones, but her cheeks still had some baby fat.

"Don't just fuckin' stand there, boy," Aunt Chrissy admonished.

Thea climbed up on the couch and tilted her head at me, and all her mannerisms came rushing back. Since she didn't speak, her body language was more expressive than most kids. It used to be, anyway. I hoped that was the case now, too.

Go to her.

There was a chair next to the couch, and I aimed for that and sat down. Thea watched me with interest. No recognition that I could see.

She looked different. Some of her freckles had faded. Her hair had gone darker, with only some hint of reddish left. I'd done the same as a kid. Fucking hell, as a toddler, I'd practically been a ginger.

"Do you remember Daddy, Thea?" Aunt Chrissy asked.

Thea looked down.

My heart shattered, but the relief of seeing her was so immense that it made things bearable. I leaned forward, resting my forearms on my knees, and I had to blink rapidly and wipe my eyes.

Thea grabbed a notepad and a pen from the coffee table.

"She still doesn't speak, does she?" I asked quietly.

My aunt shook her head. "She writes and reads, though."

"Really?" Pride filled me to the fucking brim. "How's that even possible? She's only three."

She shrugged. "Her sitter—she's a good egg. She ain't normal either, but she's explained some shit to me." She lit up a smoke. I was tempted to ask for one, but I could do that later when Thea wasn't near. "There are disorders. Willow—the sitter—thinks she's got one'a those. They call it speech impairment or whatever. Nonverbal. But she's sharp." She nodded at Thea, who was drawing something. "Willow's been teaching her this and that. And sign language."

I was amazed and completely choked up.

I grinned and wiped at my cheeks again.

"You're cute." Aunt Chrissy jerked her chin at me. "Ya big mush."

"I missed her." Saying those words nearly slayed me, and I rubbed my jaw and mouth as an excuse for not making any sounds. She saw through me, but whatever. "Fuck." I covered my face with my hands and screwed my eyes shut. Tears burned behind the lids, and my bottom lip wouldn't stop trembling.

"Aww, sweetie. You're here now. Forget this past year and move on."

It wasn't that easy, but I nodded sharply and did my best to lock up my emotions.

"I'mma go make some food," she said. "You reconnect or somethin'. Mac and cheese okay?"

"Sure." I didn't care about food, though I liked she was leaving the room.

Thea continued drawing, and I continued watching her. I tented my hands in front of my face, as if I were praying, thumbs under my chin, and I just stared. She'd changed so much, yet she was so undoubtedly her. I wanted to say something, but I didn't know what.

Our bond had never come from talking. It was touch.

It was the little things. Odd things to some, maybe. Like when I'd been sick or down in the dumps. She would nuzzle into the crook of my neck or kiss my fingertips or leave butterfly kisses along my arm. Or when she was feeling mischievous, she would head-butt me playfully and giggle like mad.

I'd been the only person who could initiate touch. She was wary—or used to be, anyway—of others, anyone invading her personal space, except for me.

Who knew where I stood now.

Thea slid off the couch after a while and eyed her drawing critically. Too fucking cute. Then she nodded to herself, and I found myself holding my breath when she came to my side and showed me the notepad.

Oh, fuck this, the waterworks were coming again.

She had drawn a ketchup bottle, and she'd written "Willow say I might got an almost ededic memory" on the paper.

A choked sound escaped me, something between a chuckle and a cry, and my day was officially made. Her misspelling of eidetic had only made it better.

"You remember me?" I grinned through my tears, and tapping her arm twice with my index finger came from muscle memory. "Jesus Christ, baby." Who the fuck was this kid? A genius. If she didn't look like me, if I hadn't taken a paternity test...I would've doubted our relation.

She nodded and broke eye contact.

"I never wanted to leave you." My words came out in a quiet rush. "I thought of you every day. I missed you so fucking much, Thea. But I had to work." I winced, the memories of everything I'd done tainting the moment. "I had to save money so I could afford to come out here—" I stopped. An explanation was worth jack shit to a three-year-old. I wasn't even sure she understood. I blew out a breath and peered at the drawing. "I'll see you every day now, I swear."

I couldn't promise I'd spend every night with her. Aunt Chrissy—she was family, and I couldn't hate her. But she was a cunt too, and I wasn't counting on her letting me stay here.

29

With my promise to Thea, though, my heart had already decided I wasn't fucking going to Seattle. Someway, somehow, I'd make a living right here in Camassia Cove.

My aunt was useless during dinner. We ate in front of the TV, and she wanted to catch up on her shows. Apparently, that was more important than indulging me and telling me shit about my daughter. All the things I'd missed.

"You're not eating much." I tapped my fork on Thea's plate. "Skin and bones."

She quirked a crooked smile and shrugged one shoulder.

She was a picky eater, I knew that much. She had some allergies, too.

Thea started signing something to me, and my face fell.

"I'm sorry, baby. I don't understand. I'll learn, though." I looked over to Aunt Chrissy. "Yo, can you please translat—"

"Shhh!" She waved a hand at me, eyes glued to the TV. "You think I got time to learn sign language? Now be quiet. I don't wanna miss anything."

I glared at the floor and clenched my jaw. It was useless to argue.

Thea tapped a finger on my arm and showed me she'd written to me instead. "Talk to Willow," it said in her cute chicken scrawl.

I nodded. "I will. Thank you, Thea, that's a great idea."

Not once during dinner did I glance at the TV. I was too busy soaking up the sight of Thea's presence. I was memorizing and cataloging her quirks—some old, some new.

I fucking ached to hug her, but she had to come to me first for that. She was particular about affection, and if I wasn't that one person for her anymore, I didn't wanna assume shit and end up scaring her.

For now, I was satisfied with watching her and being completely amazed by her brilliance. It seemed, though she lacked speech and social skills, she excelled in other things, like writing and reading. I couldn't have been prouder.

"Dominic." At long last, Aunt Chrissy turned off the TV. "Glenn will be here soon. He's...got a temper."

I raised a brow.

She sighed and took a big sip of her drink. "Don't make me say it, dammit."

Oh. She wanted me to... "Got it." I set down my bowl of mac and cheese that had gone cold, anyway. She'd always been a shitty cook. "Do you know where I can go?" I didn't look at her. I guess the sting never really lessened.

It was the same old song and dance. She attracted shitheads, and she didn't want me around them. So when she had a man over, I was gone.

"I'm sorry."

She wasn't, but it was okay. I'd deal. "No worries."

"He doesn't come home every night," she went on. "His mother is sick. He spends at least two or three nights at her house."

"God," I muttered. She hadn't changed. Still the delusional woman who believed the shit men told her. Sick mother, my ass.

"You can have the couch when he ain't here," she said.

"Okay." It hurt to leave Thea, physically hurt, but I'd suck it up. I was here now, and I'd see her tomorrow. I'd see her every goddamn day, so help me God. "Are my clothes dry?"

"I'll check." Aunt Chrissy sparked up a cig and left in a swirl of smoke.

I sighed and turned my attention back to Thea. "I gotta stay somewhere else tonight," I admitted. She nodded as if she knew. "I'll be back tomorrow, though." Another nod. My smile was unsteady. I was insecure. I wanted to ask if she *wanted* me to come back, which was a loser question. "Hey. Are you still my gangsta girl?"

She cocked her head at that. A memory jogged?

Then she smiled and held up her fist, and I could've cried—again. She did remember. I grinned back and bumped her fist gently with mine.

"Perfect. I'm glad."

Aunt Chrissy returned with my clothes and a thick blanket.

"This should keep you warm..." She put the clothes on the table.

I stared at them, internally shaking my head. She had no clue. Blankets didn't work for shit. You were more likely to heat up the blanket.

Tomorrow, I would scope out places to sleep. Garages, cars, maybe there was an abandoned building—anything that wasn't outside.

There was no grand scene when I left some ten minutes later. I'd managed to box up the mushy shit inside, and Thea had disappeared into her room after a quick wave. She didn't depend on me no more. It'd been wishful thinking she still would.

I trudged down the stairs, my senses refocusing. Now it was another night as a homeless person, and moping would get me hurt or killed.

The neighborhood was quiet. All I heard were the winds. I tugged down my beanie and stuffed the blanket down into my duffel. I had some plastic bags I could use to keep dry, so that was good.

I tried several doors to various apartment buildings, but they were all locked. For twenty minutes, I waited in case the door to an underground garage would open, but obviously it didn't. Camas was fucking dead.

I snorted and rubbed my hands together. Was I the only homeless person in Camassia Cove?

Eventually, I stopped wasting energy on finding an indoor spot, and I walked back toward Olympia Square. One alley between two buildings was narrower and deeper than the others, so I took cover in the darkness and found my bed for the night next to a Dumpster.

I looked inside it first. *Nice.* There were two cardboard boxes and some newspapers, and *that* was the shit that held warmth.

Wrapping the blanket around me, I sat down on the newspapers and pulled out one of the black garbage bags from my duffel. I squirmed my way into the bag and, lastly, spread out the pieces of cardboard.

Staying outside like this in Philly was a lot different. This town felt safer, and it couldn't be false security. Looks weren't deceiving. I could feel it. Whatever people bitched about where the district of Camas was concerned, it wasn't bad. Just fucking frigid and quiet.

My hand brushed over the pocket of my hoodie, and I remembered I'd stolen a few smokes from Aunt Chrissy. So I brought one out and lit it up, taking a long pull from it.

I leaned my head back against the wall and looked up at the sky.

There were no stars.

"Welcome home, Dominic," I whispered to myself.

3

Kings Park was a dump.

It'd been a week, and I was growing desperate for cash. I had a measly two bucks left. I hadn't eaten since the day before yesterday.

Sitting on a bench in the small park, I made sure to make eye contact with every dude who passed, but there weren't many. Even fewer were willing to pay. At this point, I was rolling in thirty bucks a day—fucking pathetic.

Frustrated and weary, I picked up the copy of the *Camassia Courier* next to me, a weekly paper that was mostly bullshit. Interviews and tourist information and reviews, but it was free and it had one page for job hunters.

I chewed on my thumbnail, scanning the ads. Again. I'd circled a handful I'd call about later. Most of them were temporary gigs. But even then, fuckers hired people with resumes and referrals. Like I had that shit?

"Hey."

My head snapped up.

"What brings you here?" he asked. Older guy, lean, married, average lumberjack Joe. He sure as fuck wasn't no cop.

I eyed him. "I think you know, but I charge."

He bobbed his head and looked out over the lawn that was surrounded by trees and boulders.

"I can make it real good for you, though," I said. "Just sayin'."

He was too tempted. "Uh, how much for you to suck me?"

I thought about it. He was here to blow a load, end of. His posture reeked of impatience, so yeah, he wanted it. I could also tell he was apprehensive. Not very assertive.

"Forty bucks," I said.

His eyes widened a bit, and he rubbed his jaw.

The trick with this kind was to be dismissive. "Take it or leave it, old man." I shrugged and turned back to my paper.

He cursed. "Fine."

I remained aloof on the outside, though I was feeling pretty fucking good internally. The heartbroken ones paid the most.

We headed over to a wooded area, and I told him he could have my number if he ever wanted my services again. He didn't answer, so I shut up and found a good spot where I sank to my knees and rubbed his crotch.

"Can I call you Martin?" he asked.

"Sure." I didn't give a fuck, but I realized I could use this. "Someone you work with?"

He averted his eyes before closing them. "Sister's husband."

"I can be Martin for you."

He groaned, getting harder. "Can I fuck you instead?"

"Seventy-five bucks."

"Okay."

I exited the park seventy-five bucks richer, two dark spots on my jeans where I'd kneeled, and the confidence that my new customer would call me soon. He'd asked for my number right after he'd thrown away the rubber.

It would be another couple hours before Aunt Chrissy's shift at the nursing home started, but I was ready to get indoors. Since I was here now, at least we didn't have to spend dough on this Willow girl as much, which was both good and bad. She was obviously good to Thea, so I hoped to be able to afford the babysitter again soon.

It meant I hadn't met Willow yet, and I needed to rectify that stat so I could learn my own daughter's language.

"Dominic?"

I frowned and turned around, wondering who the fuck knew my name here. It was Teach. He was coming from the same direction I was—the park.

"Hey." I stuck my hands into my pockets. "You really look like a teacher."

I wondered idly if the blazer under his open coat had elbow patches. His button-down was untucked from his jeans, and he wore glasses today. Black frames. Kinda fit him, actually.

"My family likes to remind me of that fact." He smiled faintly and caught up to me, but that barely there smile was gone when he looked down and saw I was wet and dirty across my knees. Didn't take a genius to figure out what I'd been up to. "Making friends?" The sarcasm in his tone wasn't lost on me.

I narrowed my eyes, irritated. "A guy's gotta make a fuckin' livin'."

"You—" He was shocked, but he hid it fairly quickly. "Dominic..." Oh, fuck that. Now he showed nothing but concern, and that disgusted me. Only pity was worse. "You don't have to do that. There are options."

I stared at him flatly. Unbelievable. *Options.*

That was something the privileged told themselves to feel better. That those living on the street had a *choice.*

37

I bit out a dry chuckle. "The fuck do you know about it?"

"Not enough," he was quick to concede. "But don't take me for a fool, either. I want to help."

I paused and pursed my lips. It was dawning on me. His deal. Oh, it all made sense now. He was the knight. Much like with the heartbroken ones, knights could be taken advantage of. Not as much 'cause their judgment wasn't as clouded, but I could definitely shake Teach down a bit.

"I get it now." I smirked. "Your youngest brother, he said you got a bleeding heart. Then the yuppie brother's comment about Camas... You guys didn't grow up here." I gestured at his clothes. "Your job, teaching in this cute version of the projects. You don't have to live in this 'hood. You *want* to." Living on the streets for years had taught me a thing or two about people. "I can go further if you want. Something probably happened when you was young. Did'ju lose someone? And ever since, you wanna save people?" I let out a laugh. I'd walk away if I could afford to turn down a buck. "No wonder you offered me a ride so quick."

To his credit, he didn't give anything away. His expression was mild, unimpressed.

"Is it my turn now?" he drawled.

Oh, this oughta be good. "Be my guest."

"All right." He gestured for us to start walking again. "Given that you saw dollar signs the second I offered to help, how about we skip the prideful bullshit of going back and forth before you agree and you let me make you dinner? Then I can tell you I have you pegged, too."

I pinched my lips together, not admitting I was a little impressed. Of-fucking-course I was starving, too. He was taller and carried some bulk under those winter clothes, but I had no doubt I was faster and could take him. So dinner should be safe. Should.

"Okay. I could eat."

"Of course you could. When was the last time you ate?"

"I've had a few good loads today."

"Now you're lying."

I frowned at the ground as we walked together toward Olympia Square. "How do you know?"

"Because there's little to no oral going on in Kings Park."

That statement was fucking ridiculous. "You talk shit."

Teach stopped me and leveled me with a look. "You don't have to share any details. In fact, I prefer you don't. But think back. You haven't given much head in this park, and if you have, it certainly hasn't given you any...*loads*." He barely masked his distaste at that.

I didn't reply. I *had* noticed very few dudes wanted head, and those who did wore condoms. Almost unheard of.

"HIV scare a couple years ago." He started walking again, and I followed. "The majority of the men who visit the park are family men, and two reported cases of contracting HIV were enough for them to use protection. But I'm sure stupidity will make them forget soon. That's how it usually goes, until the next scare."

Side-eyeing him, I wondered how he knew so much about it. It was a small town, in comparison. People were probably all up in each other's business, but he seemed *invested*.

"Was you one of the family men?" I asked.

"Were, and no. Not my scene."

"Yo, don't correct my grammar."

A smile flitted over his face. "Why, are you going to shank me?"

I snorted, but then I faltered. I wanted to make something crystal clear. "I could."

"I know." He inclined his head, staring straight ahead. "I wouldn't underestimate you, Dominic."

Good.

Adrian's apartment was just across the square from Aunt Chrissy's place. His was a bachelor pad, with the addition of books *everywhere*. He gave me the grand tour, revealing two bedrooms, a bath, and a kitchen that opened up to the living room. Books, books, books. I couldn't see his kitchen table. Judging by the stacks of papers and markers strewn all over, I could guess he'd graded some tests there in his days.

It was homey. It smelled of soap, old pages, lemon, and...food?

The walls weren't covered in peeling-off paper, nor were they yellowed by years of smoking indoors.

"Take the chicken out of the fridge and turn off the slow cooker for me, please," Teach said. "I'm going to change."

What the fuck was a slow cooker?

He disappeared down the hall, and I placed my hands on my hips, glancing around me in the kitchen. I saw some pot thing where a red lamp was on, so maybe that was it. I inched closer and lifted the lid, immediately assaulted by a smell that made my mouth water. My gut twisted in hunger.

This shit had been on all day?

It looked like marinara, but it was thicker and had chunks of vegetables and what I guessed were mushrooms in it.

I felt out of place here. It was uncomfortable as fuck, but I wasn't about to turn down a meal I'd have to sell an arm and a leg for in a restaurant.

The fridge was fully stocked. There was a pot of fresh fucking herbs on the counter. Was he a chef, too?

Opening a drawer, I grabbed a wooden spoon to try the chunky marinara, and that was how Teach found me. He grinned. I was frozen with a goddamn ladle in my mouth, but it was *him*.

"Does it pass the test?" he asked and opened the fridge.

If he was asking about the food or his body, I didn't know. He wasn't no teacher no more. He was as tatted up as his younger brother, and there was an edge to him now. I didn't like it for shit. Those kind peepers with barely visible crow's feet at the corners had deceived me, after all.

He was still wearing his jeans, but the blazer and button-down had been replaced by a wife-beater. Bare feet. Hair pushed back. That beard. And the fucking ink. It covered his arms and chest.

I swallowed and took a step back. I couldn't taste the food.

I eyed his arms. Muscular but not gym bulky. Could I really take him?

"Are you all right?" He flicked his gaze to me for a beat before he focused on the chicken. It was shredded, and he dumped it out of a Tupperware container and into a skillet on the stove.

That was a weapon.

"Yeah." I scanned every inch of the kitchen. My blade had nothing on the knives in the stand on the counter, so I'd have to stay close to them.

"Dominic." Teach faced me with a patient, almost gentle expression. Fuck that. Fuck those eyes. "I'm not going to hurt you."

I laughed. "You couldn't."

Except, he could.

Teach stared at me pensively, but in the end, he turned his back on me and paid more attention to cooking than me.

He was purposely ignoring me.

It helped.

When I moved closer to the knife stand, he was merely humming and stirring in the chicken. He added butter and broke off some leaves from his plant of herbs.

By the time the food was done, I'd mapped out enough escape routes and ways to defend myself for any number of reasons and attack methods that I was feeling better. Calmer. Prepared.

Teach gave me a plate full of that chunky sauce, chicken, and pasta, and I eye-fucked it on the way to the living room where we sat down.

I was practically salivating. I couldn't remember ever seeing anything so fancy within my grasp.

"I'm glad you joined me, Dominic."

There was no time to look at him. My fork went between my plate and my mouth. I understood food porn now. "Why?" I gathered the next mouthful on my fork. The chicken was amazing. It wasn't very often I got to eat meat.

He chuckled. "It beats eating alone, of course."

Oh. Yeah, maybe. Depended how you looked at it. When you were safe, perhaps company was nicer. When you were digging through a Dumpster, you sure as fuck didn't want anyone sneaking up on ya.

"So you said you have me pegged." I waved my fork at him. "Amaze me, Teach."

"Isn't my cooking doing that for me?" He smirked.

"Fuckin' delicious," I agreed. "Now, shoot."

He laughed kindly and removed his glasses. "Fair enough." He rubbed his eyes a bit, as if he were tired. He probably was. I couldn't imagine working with teenagers. Fuck that. "You've lived on the streets, yes?"

I swallowed my food, staring at the plate. "Yeah. That obvious, huh?"

"Quite."

I nodded and reached for my glass of milk. "I get it. I hadn't showered in a while when I met you and your brothers in Seattle."

"It was more than that." He paused to take a swig of his beer. "You're constantly ready for battle. You're jumpy, defensive, and in survival mode. It says a thing or two about your past."

"Hmm." I hadn't considered that.

He continued. "Which leads me to believe it's been your life for quite some time."

"On and off since I was fifteen." My plate was almost empty, and it was a good thing. I'd eaten too fast and knew a stomachache was coming. "First my pop kicked the bucket when I was eleven, and then my mom when I was fourteen."

"I'm sorry to hear that." He was quiet for a beat, maybe to gauge my mood before he went on. It was nothing to me, though. People died. End of. "I take it you were placed with family?"

I narrowed my eyes. "My dad's sister."

He must've noticed my suspicion, so he explained. "You mentioned you had family here." Oh, right. "It indicates you haven't been completely alone. Furthermore, those placed in the system rarely return to foster care once they've run away, and you said you've been homeless on and off."

Damn, the fucker was on the ball.

"Aight." I drank some more of my milk and saw I had to go soon. Aunt Chrissy would be leaving for work in half an hour. "So how do you know about this shit? You've never lived on the street."

"No, I have not." He leaned back in his chair, finished with his meal. "I went to college on the East Coast, and I met some amazing people who worked with runaways and LGBT youth who had been kicked out of their homes. It made a big impact and changed a lot about who I was. More importantly, who I became."

I could sense there was more to the story. When he spoke, he did so with conviction and eye contact. But he'd looked away when he told me that, so I wondered if maybe I was right earlier. When I asked if he'd lost someone.

This unsettled me. I'd gotten to know Billy right after Aunt Chrissy and I moved down to Philly three years ago. Whenever she asked me to leave, he was there. But I hadn't trusted him—far from it. That had taken a year or so. Two years before I could relax being in the same room with him when no one else was there.

He was one of those people who actually gave a fuck. He'd done it all: community centers, youth groups, neighborhood watch, Big Brother programs, rehab for kids... He didn't say anything. He just *did*. He showed and proved he was a good guy.

They were the people who blurred the lines for me, 'cause it was easy to mistrust everyone. It was easy to think all adults had ulterior motives or they were full of shit or they lied. Whatever. Except those fucking people.

Was Teach one of them?

I bit my lip.

"You're staying with family now, right?" he asked.

I lifted one shoulder. "Sometimes."

"I see." And he probably did. If he had experience with what I was going through, it made sense that he didn't frown or go nuts, because he knew the reality. Not every family was whole-some. Adrian looked to me, thoughtful, a little resigned. "You wouldn't accept an offer of staying here, would you?"

I shook my head. No fucking way. I'd have to let my guard down—sleep in a stranger's home with only him around? No, thanks.

"You'd be a stupid motherfucker to make that offer," I told him.

He didn't know me. I could rob him blind. Stab him in his sleep. Like he could do with me.

"I've made some foolish decisions before," he admitted. "I don't think this would be one of them."

"Why not?"

He stood up with his plate, and he grabbed mine, too. "I saw you the other day."

I followed him to the kitchen and gave him my glass.

"You were coming out of the grocery store with a pack of diapers."

"So?" I stiffened.

He smiled faintly as he started doing the dishes. "Gut instinct, perhaps. But I think you have someone you care about enough to stay out of trouble." He paused. "I'll be blunt. You're an orphan—a homeless one, at that. You put yourself at risk by selling sex, and the harsh reality is that most young people who do that do it to pay for expensive drugs. But you don't show any signs of addiction whatsoever."

When he tossed me a dish towel, I grabbed a plate and dried it absent-mindedly.

"What's the going rate for a blow job these days?"

I shot him a scowl, and he laughed.

"I was joking." He grinned and turned off the faucet, then leaned his hip against the counter and folded his arms over his chest. The amusement was gone, leaving room for understanding. "I won't ask why you're exchanging sex for money, Dominic. I can guess. If you were on your own, you would, at the very least, be able to afford a crappy motel room. You'd have food in your stomach."

I nodded and looked down, uncomfortable as fuck.

"But you're not on your own, are you?" he asked rhetorically. "You have someone to provide for, and minimum wage wouldn't get you very far."

Dead on.

It was a goal of mine to find a legit job that could pay for me and Thea, but I was stuck. I'd fallen between the cracks the day I was born, basically. I was entitled to some help, fucking obviously, but then I'd also risk losing custody of my daughter. If some social worker came to investigate, they'd see me—a goddamn bum—my aunt who sure as fuck wasn't fit to be a guardian, and Thea. Thea, a three-year-old little girl who, on paper, would count as a special-needs kid.

"I gotta go," I said lamely. The air was becoming stifling in here, and I felt exposed. "Thanks for the grub, Teach."

"One thing, Dominic." He walked ahead of me to the hall-way, and once there, he picked up a key from the bowl on the hallway table. "It's a spare key to my car."

My brows knitted together. "I don't drive."

The corners of his mouth twitched. "I remember." Then he reached out for my hand, and I flinched and tensed up, but he ignored it and placed the key in my palm. "It's a dry place to sleep. You know what my car looks like. It's parked behind the building, and I have a feeling you can jump a fence."

I stared at the key and chewed on my lip. "Am I a pet project or some fucking charity case?" I wasn't pissed or anything. I only wanted to know what he was doing. What he got outta this.

"Call it whatever the fuck you want." Teach used the F word. "When I can help, I will. Standing by and doing nothing while humanity becomes uglier isn't for me."

"Deep," I muttered.

He sighed. "I believe the words you're looking for are *thank you*."

I couldn't help but grin at him. "'Thank you."

"Better." He opened the door. "Listen, I volunteer at the Camas Quad on Thursdays. It's a youth center and a safe place for kids who don't like being at home." He snatched up a business card from the table and gave it to me. "You're not a kid, but you're more than welcome to stop by. If getting help to find a job or speaking to a counselor doesn't appeal, perhaps a hot meal and making friends will."

I nodded slowly, unsure of what to say. It was a lot of information. A lot of help.

"My number's on that card too."

"Okay." I stepped out of the apartment, feeling awkward. "Thanks. For..." I waved a hand. *Everything.*

"Anytime."

4

I grinned and ran a towel over my head as I checked the drawings Thea had made today. She was skilled as fuck, and she obviously loved it. It was her language, in a way.

As the days passed, she was growing more and more comfortable around me, and every time she relaxed a bit more, I was fucking mush. Done for. Tears would fall the second she'd gone to bed.

"What's this?" I pointed to one of the drawings.

She reached for the notepad on the coffee table and scribbled, "Symmetry."

"Okay, I'm off to work." Aunt Chrissy emerged from the bathroom. "Glenn won't be home, so the couch is yours, hon."

"Aight." That made me happy. I'd spent the past four in Teach's car, so it'd be nice to stretch out.

I'd met Glenn once, in passing. Let's just say I wasn't fond of the fucker. He ignored Thea completely, acted as if she didn't exist, though that was almost preferable to the alternative. He could've been abusive, in which case he wouldn't be breathing now.

"Was it tonight Willow was comin' over?" my aunt asked.

I nodded.

"Are you a mute now, too?" She snorted. "Anyway, you got some cash? I'm short."

I frowned at her. "I gave you sixty yesterday."

She flashed me an impatient look and pocketed her bus pass. "Look, I don't gotta explain myself to you, Dominic. I work full time to support your kid—"

"Don't go there." I gave her a warning look. My voice was calm, but I'd flip my shit on her if she pushed it. "If I was you, I wouldn't cut off the hand that feeds me—or, in your case, pays for the booze. So let's get one thing straight. I pay for Thea, myself, your addiction, and almost half the rent. Quit pickin' up Glenn's bar tabs."

"You got a lotta nerve." She shook her head and put on her coat. "Speaking of cutting off hands, how about I toss your ungrateful ass out? Huh? What if I told you to take Thea with you?"

In that moment, I despised my aunt.

Thea had grown quiet and completely still. I remembered doing the same as a kid when my folks were fighting and throwing things at each other. It pained me to have her in this situation. It made me physically ill to be part of it. I was a bum-ass dad.

"There's a twenty in my hoodie," I said quietly.

"Thank you." Aunt Chrissy left after taking half of what I owned. I'd been hoping to take Thea to McDonald's or something, but I had to buy groceries, too. She was running low on coloring books as well, and that was one of those things I refused to let my girl go without.

After a moment of silence, Thea grabbed my hand and spelled out "Daddy" across my palm with her finger.

It made me smile like a fool.

I kissed her hand and then brought it to my heart. *Always, baby.*

Thea squealed and clapped her hands when Willow arrived, and I couldn't help but chuckle at her. She bounced after me as I let Willow in, after which I became somewhat of a spectator for a beat.

Willow was a shortie and looked like one of those emo girls. Her hair was shoulder-length, straight, and black. Her skin was alabaster. But she was cute, I guessed. Around my age, maybe a little younger. She wore a pretty smile for Thea, the two talking animatedly in sign language.

"Thank you for coming," I said.

Willow straightened and nodded politely, and then she dug out a stack of Post-its.

I'd emailed with her, so I knew she didn't speak, either. Or rather, she wouldn't talk to me for a while—until she got comfortable. Apparently, it was an anxiety issue.

She had explained she wasn't really a babysitter. I'd felt that I'd found a confidant when she had told me how she'd become Thea's closest friend. Some seven months ago, Willow had met Aunt Chrissy and Thea at the store. My aunt had been her inconsiderate self and hadn't given a fuck about Thea's own anxiety issues. My girl had been freaking out over something, and Willow had intervened. After that, she'd felt compelled to protect Thea.

I remembered laughing at Willow's one comment about people. "I dislike humans in general, but I couldn't not do anything."

Humans.

As if she wasn't one herself.

We ended up in the living room, and I apologized for not having anything to offer her but water.

She waved it off. Then she opened her backpack and pulled out heaps of folders, books, and notepads. It was the beginning of what would turn into an hour-long mindfuck for me.

Willow was single-focused in her quest to inform and educate, and it was overwhelming. So many words I'd never heard before. Medical terms, disorders, spectrums, shit about underdevelopment and overdevelopment, selective mutism, texture issues, fixations, quirks... She both signed and showed me written-down stuff; there was a lot of gesturing, and I would need hours and hours alone to go through it all again.

But I was determined. Funnily enough, I'd never really missed Thea not speaking. We used our little touches to convey many things, though I was definitely planning on learning ASL as fast as possible.

"You have to find a balance," one of Willow's notes said. "Learning alternative ways to communicate will make her comfortable, but it's important she doesn't get lazy. Keep the goal in mind. We want her to speak eventually, if it's a possibility for her."

I nodded. That was understandable.

Willow's hand had to hurt. While she had prepared a lot before she got here, she was still adding things on notes for me, and she did it rapidly as fuck.

I waited, studying a list of traits. I recognized Thea in a lot of them, and my brow furrowed as I watched her now. She was signing something to Willow, something I'd seen her sign multiple times before. Her hand was closed, except for her index finger, and she used it to tap her temple three times.

"What's she saying?" I asked Willow.

Willow looked up from her notepad and tilted her head at Thea. Then she smiled and scribbled to me on a note.

"She's saying 'That's my daddy' over and over, and she's given you a sign name," it said.

I grinned, my chest filling with warmth. "A sign name?"

Willow explained it was a personal nickname in sign language. Instead of spelling a name out letter by letter, people created their own names. And Thea had made one for me. It was the one I'd seen her do but hadn't understood. Closed fist with the index finger extended was the letter "D" for Daddy, and she tapped it three times to her temple as an *I love you.*

I stared down at the slip of paper Willow had explained it on and felt my cheeks heating up. My vision becoming blurry came next, and I clenched my jaw. *Holy fuck.* I swallowed hard.

"Thea..." I cleared my throat and patted my thigh. She looked to me curiously and climbed up on my lap, and I closed my eyes and pressed my forehead to hers. "I'm gonna hug you, okay?"

She nodded, and I slowly wrapped my arms around her little frame.

"I love you," I whispered. "So, so, so much." I pressed gentle kisses over her forehead, hair, cheeks, and nose.

Thea grinned crookedly.

She was pretty quick to get outta my grasp and get back her personal space, but I didn't care. As overwhelming as this education was, it was shaping up to be one of the best nights of my life.

From that day on, wherever I went, I brought something to study. Willow had provided me with a lot of information, and she said I could borrow her textbooks for as long as I needed. It came in handy when I had long, cold nights ahead of me in Adrian's car.

Tonight was one of those nights. It was around midnight, snow was coming down heavily, and I hadn't been here long enough to get warm. I got as comfortable as possible, thanks to a certain teacher's *gifts*, and rubbed my hands together.

There was always something new waiting for me in the backseat. The best part was the sleeping bag. A solid one, made for camping in cold weather. It was the first thing I slipped into when I got in.

One night, I'd found a pillow and a flashlight. Then I'd started seeing candy bars and bottled water sticking up from the pocket on the back of the passenger seat.

Tonight, there'd been a pair of gloves and a thick scarf.

Fucker.

My mind strayed as I studied a text about speech practice. Part of me was trying to focus on the fact that there was a possibility Thea might speak one day. The other part of me couldn't help but wonder if Adrian was like Billy.

I'd spoken briefly to Billy last week when he called about my test results. He didn't have much to say, mainly because at that point, Teach and I had only shared that first dinner. But also 'cause Billy said explaining shit to me was like talking to a brick wall. I was gonna believe people were bad no matter what he said.

Maybe he was wrong, maybe he was right.

Either way, I got his message. He still saw good in people. He had faith and whatever. He thought I should give Teach a chance and "make some damn friends."

Friends. Foreign concept to me nowadays.

I jumped at the quiet "tap, tap, tap" on the window and froze, eyes wide. Speak of the fucking devil. It was Teach, and he unlocked the door and got in behind the wheel, his legs sticking out.

"Sorry to intrude." He was lit. Not a lot, but I had a radar for alcohol levels, and he'd had a few. "How are you?"

"Good." I was still trying to calm the fuck down, my heart pounding. "What're you doing up?"

He smiled and removed his beanie. "Just came home from a birthday dinner with my little brother and his girlfriend. I saw you were here, and I have leftovers." He held up a plastic bag. "Interested?"

I smiled hesitantly and accepted the bag. "Whose birthday?" Peering inside, I saw it was Chinese leftovers and a fork from his place. "Thank you. I love Chinese food."

"You're welcome."

I dug in right away. It was lukewarm but tasted awesome. "Whose birthday, drunkard?"

"Oh." He snorted a chuckle. "Mine. And I'm not drunk."

"Your eyes are glassy, birthday boy." I watched him, amused. A bit wary, but it wasn't too bad. "So how old are you now?"

"Thirty-five going on fifty-five."

I smirked. He did carry himself older than he was, but he didn't necessarily *look* older. Especially not when the boring teacher attire came off and he showed off his ink and his body.

"Well, happy fuckin' birthday, Teach." I shoveled some noodles and shrimp into my mouth. "I'm afraid I don't got shit to give you unless you want a blow job."

The food made me hum appreciatively. Having only had some milk and cereal this morning, it came at a perfect time—before I had the chance to fill my stomach with chocolate.

"Jesus, Dominic. Tell me you're joking." Teach was shaking his head, baffled.

I frowned. "What? It's just head. You don't even gotta be queer to enjoy it."

"Lord," he muttered. "I don't know what to say."

He was making a big deal outta nothing, as far as I was

concerned. I shrugged and went back to eating, but now I was curious.

"Are you queer?"

He sighed. "I'm gay. Yes."

"You got a man?" I chewed on a piece of shrimp.

"No."

For some reason, this was a sore topic for him. I could tell. His expression was guarded, and he was all stiff in his posture. Fucking weirdo.

"Well..." I shrugged again. "You've given me a lot, and it's your birthday, so..."

"I'm not helping you for sexual favors," he said irritably.

"I didn't say you were! Mother of Christ, you're uptight," I laughed. "If you're worried about STDs—"

"That's always a concern, and it should be for you, as well." He was in lecturing mode. The teacher peepers were coming out. Stern, firm. "The mere thought of you risking your health..." He shook his head and looked down.

My mirth faded. There was a story there.

"My bad." I closed the container, saving the rest for breakfast in the morning. "I'm clean, though. I haven't done anything unprotected since last time I got tested, and I don't do bareback anymore. Haven't in a year."

"That's only reassuring for the minute." His smile was sarcastic before he looked away. "I can't believe we're discussing this. But while we're on the subject, what about you? Are you gay? I won't make assumptions based on what you do. There aren't exactly many women who buy sex on the street."

I lifted one shoulder. "I don't know. Sex isn't sexual for me."

"That's...fucking painful to hear, Dominic." He gave a slow shake of his head. "I admire you. I really do. I won't even pretend to think I would've survived in your situation, but I wish you knew..." He trailed off.

I didn't reply.

I knew I was fucked up and stunted in some ways. People thought I was stupid, but I wasn't. I knew theory, I knew there were other realities, *I knew*. I knew right from wrong. I knew sex was supposed to be intimate; I'd just never experienced it.

I'd discovered that sex had a price before I even lost my virginity.

"Will you come up for dinner this weekend?" Adrian asked. "I'd like to discuss something with you."

"Sure. I have time before then, too."

"I work late tomorrow, and I have plans with my brothers on Friday, but how about Saturday?"

I nodded. "Okay."

5

On Saturday, I arrived at Teach's place around seven, and he was making homemade pizza and had some acoustic rock music playing in the background.

He didn't look like a teacher tonight. Black basketball shorts, another white beater, a ball cap on backward, and all those tattoos made him look like anything *but* a teacher.

"Help me slice the mushrooms?" He slid over a cutting board and a knife.

I'd never really cooked, unless you counted mac and cheese, omelets, and noodles. But hey, I could give it a go.

He was chopping up onions and what he told me were garlic greens, and I side-eyed him every now and then to see if I could mirror his technique. I failed, but whatever.

It was while paying attention to what he did that the designs of his ink caught my eye for the first time. Not as a red flag warning about bad guys, gang members, or anyone with an *edge*. But as art. And I had to grin. The tattoo covering his right shoulder and the better part of his bicep was a battle from the Civil War. It bled into the next tattoo on his forearm, which was a 1300s European plague doctor wearing the infamous beaked mask. The details were cool. From potions and open medical books to smoke from cannons and facial expressions of Union soldiers frozen in a war cry.

"You're a nerd," I told him.

"Huh?" He glanced to where I was looking and smiled. "Oh, yes. Loud and proud."

I snorted, though I couldn't hide my amusement. It was sorta sweet, I guessed.

"Kinda crazy," I said, slicing the last mushroom as thinly as I could. "The Black Death claimed, what, a third of Europe's population? Today we cure it with antibiotics."

"Or use it as biological warfare." Teach glanced at me, curious. "Are you interested in history?"

I shrugged. "I like to read."

Books were a healthy drug. They could sweep me away from storms, make me forget bruises, and soothe any emotional ache, if only for a moment. History was full of fascinating tales of guts and glory, each one a vacation I could afford.

"Billy gave me a book about the witch trials once. I liked that one a lot."

Teach smiled, a lazy one that tugged more on the left side of his mouth. "I'll be damned. Who's Billy?"

I told him while we put a bunch of fixings on the rolled-out crust. Tomato sauce, fresh spinach, mushrooms, onion, Serrano ham, mozzarella, oregano... I trailed off when Teach was about to add olives.

"Do you mind if we do a corner without olives?" I asked uncertainly.

"Not a fan?"

I shifted on my feet. "It's not for me. I was...wondering if I could bring a small piece to someone."

Thea's diet seriously sucked, and I wanted to introduce her

to more foods. There was so little she ate as it was. Olives, I knew, made her gag. But maybe she'd like the rest.

"Oh, of course you can." Teach avoided a generous piece when he applied the olives. "This someone. Would that be the little one you bought diapers for? A sister?"

I shook my head and licked the pad of my thumb, tasting garlic and tomato. "Daughter." I opened the oven as he picked up the pan, and he faltered in his movement slightly.

"You have a daughter?"

"Yeah." I brought out my phone with the cracked screen and showed him the background. It had been taken recently. Thea and I'd had a snowball fight on our way home from the playground. "Thea. She's three."

Teach smiled softly. "She's adorable."

I nodded and stepped back while he put the pizza in the oven.

"How long were you away from her?"

"A year." I hated thinking about it. Everything I'd missed.

"I can't even imagine." He opened the fridge and grabbed a beer for himself, and he gave me a look in question.

"Milk?" I asked.

He grinned to himself and poured me a glass, and then we walked into the living room. He sat down in his chair, so I went for the couch like last time.

This was dangerous in a way, 'cause I was getting comfortable around Adrian. There was an air about him. He radiated comfort and warmth. *Not safe.* But I wasn't sure I had the energy to keep my guard up at full force. It was exhausting to doubt everyone.

"Does it bother you if I drink alcohol?" He motioned to his beer.

I shook my head. "Not at all." And because the motherfucker made me feel comfortable, I told him that my folks had loved booze a bit too much, particularly my dad. It wasn't for me, but like I'd said, I didn't mind when others drank. As long as they weren't shitfaced.

"That's never me," he assured.

He didn't need to give me any reassurances, though. It wasn't an issue.

"You wanted to discuss somethin'," I said.

He inclined his head and sat forward. "Do you know how many homeless people we have in the district of Camas?"

"No."

"Nine, though a significantly larger number is currently in emergency housing."

That number was cute when you were from New York, but Camas wasn't that big.

"Okay. I've only seen one other bum." I wiped my mouth and set down my glass on the table. "Some drunk in the park. What's your point?"

"I don't want you to be number ten."

I raised a brow. "Looks like I already am."

"But we can *change* that, Dominic." He leveled me with a look, patient yet determined. "Please be honest now. Do you believe I pose a threat to you? Do you think I would take advantage of you? Hurt you in your sleep?"

"Some have before."

"I have no doubt," he replied softly. He had a crease of worry in his forehead. "The way you tense up says more than I can take."

Trouble was, I believed him. It bothered me like hell. He'd shown nothing but kindness and generosity toward me, from the moment he offered me a ride to now. Giving me food, shelter, understanding... But that could be ripped away from me.

I pinched my bottom lip, my knee bouncing.

"My main concern is getting you off the streets and away

from prostitution," he said. "I can offer a room and food for both you and your daughter. Rent free. On two conditions."

No words left me. I was physically unable to form a word. My mind was a jumbled mess, 'cause what he had to offer, I guessed, were things I hadn't even seen on the horizon.

"One," he went on, "you don't sell your body again. You go through a full physical, so I can relax, knowing you're safe—"

"You're obsessed with testing," I blurted out.

He nodded. "I admit, I am. I can tell you why later." He paused. "And two, you'll let me put you to work. I take pride in being part of a community that wants to clean up our neighborhood, and we always need more help."

Basically, I would feel like a real citizen and become a part of society instead of living on the outside and constantly trying to get a peek inside. I'd be part of a community.

I swallowed hard, and my knee bounced faster.

It was too good to be true.

"What's the catch?" My throat closed up, so I coughed into my fist. "I get to live with my daughter—away from my aunt— and I get to wake up in the morning knowing I don't gotta bend over at some point that day." It was unbelievable. "If you say I gotta go to therapy, I'll beat your ass."

He let out a chuckle and shook his head. "No. If, one day, you want to at least talk to someone—try it out—no one will be happier than me, but I know the stock you're created from. You compartmentalize and rationalize and move on. You're a tough make, Dominic." He picked up his beer and played with the label. "I want...conversation, I suppose. I'm interested in your views and your perspective. I think we can learn a lot from one another."

That wasn't a catch. I couldn't remember a time I sat down and talked to someone like equals.

"I want to," I confessed, "but I've been let down before. No one starts out thinking you're on your own."

"Very true." He pursed his lips in thought. "You know what? Forget what I said about volunteering. If you get a day off, I can drag you down to the Quad to help out. What I really should help you with is finding a paying job. That way, you won't have to depend on me for long."

I opened my mouth then closed it again. A real job? Was he some kind of fuckin' wizard now, too? "How? No one would hire me. Trust, I've tried."

"I get the impression you're not very picky, so it won't be a problem," he assured me. "You leave that to me."

"Aight..." I thought he was nuts, but whatever. The kindest nut in history.

The timer went off in the kitchen, and Teach gave me a minute to myself while he checked the pizza.

My *yes* was on the tip of my tongue, and it was the weary kid in me who had no fight left. But I was a grown man. I wanted to know more about Adrian before I left the deep end of the pool, in which I'd been slowly drowning for years, and took a step toward shallower waters.

Dinner came with lighter topics. Maybe Teach knew I needed to process, so he gave me a break and told me a bit about the town. He clearly loved his job, and I was curious. I wanted to see him in his element, surrounded by high school kids the likes of which I would no doubt end up murdering after a single class.

I was one of those who hated school but loved learning. It had to be on my own time. I'd failed most classes before I'd dropped out. But at home, when I had one, I could read for hours and forget what day or season it was.

"You could've been a chef," I said, biting into a slice of pizza. "Instead, you picked teaching."

He laughed quietly. "Well, the way I see it... Give a man a fish, and he's fed for a day. Teach him how to fish, and he's fed for life."

I'd heard that before. Knowledge was power and so on.

"As fond as I am of cooking, it's only a hobby," he said. "I grow herbs and vegetables out there when the weather permits it." He nodded at the door to the fire escape. "But education surpasses everything."

"Because you're a nerd," I said with a nod.

"Punk." He rolled his eyes.

I grinned.

"How old are you, anyway?" he asked. "It's never too late to go back to school."

"Fuck that. I'm twenty-four." I finished my pizza and set down the plate. "All I really want is a regular job and a roof over my head. If I one day can send Thea to college, that'd be great. But it's not for me."

His eyes sparked with interest. "Tell me about your daughter."

"Nuh-uh." I shook my head, sly. "Another time. You tell me why you're obsessed with safe sex."

"You mean besides the obvious reasons?" he drawled. "Fine." He wiped his hands on a napkin, done with his meal, too. "You wondered if I'd lost someone. That's correct. I befriended a girl in college. She had the biggest heart and worked her ass off at the youth center where we volunteered. She was the best friend one could possibly imagine, but her taste in men left a lot to be desired." A flicker of pain flashed across his features, and he looked down. "She was so naïve, despite knowing the dangers. Despite seeing them every day when we worked."

He got lost in a memory, and I didn't push.

I had seen my fair share of bad results coming back. I'd gotten lucky. I'd tested positive for chlamydia once, a few years ago, and then Billy had literally beaten sense into me. He'd smacked me around and shouted hard facts. It might've been the day he earned my respect.

I'd seen teenagers testing positive for far worse, though. You could see the moment the news settled and something died in their eyes.

"A boyfriend gave her HIV." Teach gathered our plates and utensils. "She was devastated but in love with a lie about what was meant to be, so she refused treatment and lived destructively. A few years after coming home from college, I flew back to attend her funeral." He stood up and brought the dishes to the kitchen, and I didn't know if I was about to follow or to give him space.

If it were me, I would want space. I just wasn't so sure Teach was like me in that respect. He seemed like a people person, and I found myself wanting to be a friend and offer... whatever I could. I'd give comfort a go.

Adrian had his back to me in the kitchen, hands planted on the counter, head hanging low.

"You aight?" I approached slowly, giving him plenty of time to tell me to fuck off.

"Yes." His voice wasn't rougher than his usual rich tone, so I didn't think he was being mushy.

I joined him and ran a hand through my hair. "Sorry about your friend. She should've been smarter. I know that's rude as fuck. Sorry."

He didn't move from his position, except tilting his head my way, and his mouth twitched. "She should have been. Question now is, will you be smarter?"

"Ouch, Teach." I placed a hand over my heart and fell back a step, pretending to be wounded. "You hit where it hurts."

His eyes flashed with wry amusement, and he shook his head at me. "I'm being serious."

I knew that. I sighed and scratched my ear. "Give me a few days to think about it?"

That didn't satisfy him. I knew his line of thought. Where my survival mode made me see dollar signs and ways to get outta my current situation, he saw a number of sexual encounters that could give me HIV. He was a drama queen.

"Stubborn." He huffed out a breath and stared at my hand that rested on the counter. "Can't I lend you money?"

I didn't understand him. Why did he care *so much?*

"This is different." I waved a hand between us. "Asking you for money would make me feel like shit." I felt vulnerable just thinking about that. "You're already offering food and a place to stay, but say you find me a job. It's gonna be another month before I can actually pull my weight, and—"

Teach straightened and took a step toward me, almost as if he was gonna hug me or some crap, but he didn't. He shook his head and told me that was the last thing he wanted, for me to feel bad.

My main issue had shifted, though. I wasn't really listening. He kept talking, but now that hug was in my head.

I remembered my mom hugging me sometimes. Other than that...?

I nodded absently, pretending to be listening to Adrian, and tried to think back. Had I hugged anyone other than Thea since my mother had died? That was ten years ago.

Would it bring comfort, the way it was intended, or would I panic and feel cornered?

"Dominic?"

My head snapped up. "Huh? Yeah, sounds good."

He smirked. "You didn't hear a word of what I said."

Whoops? "My bad. A lot on my mind. You were saying?"

Teach looked discouraged. "I'm pushing you too hard, aren't I? I apologize—"

"No, you're not," I interrupted. "I'm the one being cunty. I don't know why you're different. If it'd been someone else, I woulda jumped at the first opportunity." I guessed I wanted what he'd mentioned earlier. Conversation like equals. Mooching off him wouldn't get me there. I'd feel inferior. "Fuck." I pinched the bridge of my nose.

I had to jump. I'd dragged my shame through the mud before. This was nothing, except that I apparently valued Adrian's opinion of me. No idea how that had happened.

"Okay." I gave up. My hands fell to my sides, and I stared at the floor. "I'll never be able to repay you for literally saving me, but I can return every penny I borrow. I'm in. I accept. No need to think shit over." I swallowed the lump in my throat and glanced up warily.

We wouldn't be equals *yet*, but dammit, one day.

I'd work my ass off. Uh, legally.

Teach was pleased as punch. "You may not believe me, but you made my day."

No, I didn't believe that. Crazy son of a bitch.

One I was moving in with.

Holy shit. My heart slammed against my ribcage. I was leaving my aunt.

"I don't want this to be awkward."

"It doesn't have to be." He hummed and pulled out his wallet. "First thing tomorrow morning, I'll help you get settled in your new room. Now—" He faced me, two fingers dipping into a stack of bills. "How much do you need a week?"

I shifted my weight from foot to foot. "I don't know." I'd never done the math without having to include Aunt Chrissy. "I guess food for me and Thea is around thirty? She has some allergies and texture issues, so her food is a bit more expensive."

I couldn't make eye contact. Unbidden, I thought back on my last night in Philly when I'd begged for money from that sadistic bastard, and I knew. This was worse. This was mortifying.

"I guess a bus pass couldn't hurt if I'm gonna work," I said, biting my thumbnail. "Actually, scratch that. I can steal a bike—"

"*Dominic.*"

"What? Oh, right." I backtracked at the sight of his wide-eyed look. Weird, though. He looked like he was close to laughing his ass off, too. "Never mind. That's against the law. I know that."

Moron. It became too much for Teach, and he broke down in laughter. Meanwhile, I stood there like a fucking idiot. And I was *blushing.*

"Jesus fucking Christ," he laughed, slapping his thigh. "Oh, come here, you little shit." He did the unthinkable. Before I could react, he yanked me close for a tight hug.

I almost drop-kicked him out of instinct, but instead, I went rigid. His kind chuckles reverberated through his body, and I felt the tremors. It was warm. It was a *friend* hug. He clapped me on the back and then released me. That was it. I hadn't had any time to consider if I actually liked it. I only registered that it was colder now.

"How about this," he suggested, eyes still filled with mirth, "I leave money on the hallway table, and you take what you need. If you feel you must repay me, keep track of what you borrow and pay me back whenever. Deal?"

Still reeling from my first hug with someone who wasn't two shits high, I merely nodded and looked away. For so long, my sad excuse for a life had been the same. Get money, find shelter, bend over, fight, hunt down food, suck cock, money, bend over, shelter, fight, food. I'd gotten used to it. I guessed I had some patterns to break, and...enter this goddamn history teacher. He shook everything up.

I should say something, though I didn't know what. He was my roommate now, right? Fucked *up*. He was lending me money. He'd hugged me.

"'Teach?"

"Yeah?"

"It's awkward."

He snorted a chuckle.

6

"Excuse me?" Aunt Chrissy shrieked, tying her robe. "You're doin' *what?*"

"Pipe down!" Glenn yelled from their bedroom. "The fuck's he doing here?"

She closed the door, cutting off his bitching about me.

So much for leaving before my aunt woke up.

"We're moving," I repeated.

I'd packed what little Thea and I owned in two duffels and one black garbage bag. Now I only had to wake her up, and then we could go.

Against Adrian's wishes, I had spent last night in his car. I'd needed more time to process, and I was glad I had gotten outta his joint when I did. He made me believe things. The biggest one being a brighter future. Dangerous shit.

"You can't be serious," Aunt Chrissy hissed.

"Quiet," I snapped, opening the door to Thea's room.

She was already up. Sitting up in bed, she yawned and rubbed the sleep out of her eyes. I smiled at the bedhead she was sporting. Her curls stood everywhere.

"Mornin', gangsta." I sat down on the edge of the bed, ignoring my aunt in the doorway.

Thea signed a "good morning" in return and climbed up in my lap. I'd learned six phrases and words in ASL so far. Good morning was one of them.

"We're moving today." I smiled at her, all while she showed nothing but confusion as she glanced around and saw I had packed the few toys she owned, as well as all her coloring books. "You and me. We're going to live with a friend."

Aunt Chrissy scoffed.

Thea reached for the notepad next to her pillow, and I figured I could get shit over with where my aunt was concerned.

"Not much else to say." I shrugged. "I'll be renting a room for me and Thea at a friend's place. He's hooking me up with work, too."

She gnashed her teeth together and pointed at me. "Does this friend of yours know you deal drugs and steal to get money? Huh? I bet when he finds out, he'll kick you out, and then what? What're you gonna do then? Come running back to me? I don't fucking think so."

I stared at her flatly. She knew nothing. Me dealing drugs was laughable. That's what she got for assuming. She never questioned where I got money from, or cared. As long as she got it.

"Anyway..." I lifted my brows and looked back to Thea. "We'll be gone in ten minutes."

"What about money?"

I frowned at her. "What about it?"

"Well, you owe me, Dominic—"

I cut her off with a laugh. "Get the fuck outta hea' with that shit."

My aunt began ranting furiously and gesturing all over the fucking place, but I tuned her out to focus on Thea.

She bit her lip anxiously and showed me what she'd written. "Will I be alone?" she was asking.

I wasn't sure I understood, but I shook my head. Why would she be alone? "No, you'll be with me. You and I will share a room. Won't that be fun?" I wove my fingers through her hair and combed out a few knots. "We'll have a sleepover every night," I chuckled. "And Willow will be there when I work."

She nodded slowly, visibly anxious, but I'd do my best to make our new home good for her. Hella lot better than here.

Thea flinched and tensed up when Aunt Chrissy raised her voice further, and I'd fucking had it. I picked Thea up and went into the bathroom to get her outta her Pull-Up.

Her needing a diaper during the day depended on her stress and anxiety levels, so I figured it was safest to get her into a new one. Otherwise, she mostly used them at night.

"You need quiet time, baby?" I noticed she was shutting down a bit. It worried me, but I'd read about it, and Willow had mentioned shutdown mode. A way to defend herself mentally while she processed everything going on around her.

She nodded jerkily, so I assured her she didn't have to communicate until she was ready. I'd take care of everything, and I wouldn't leave her for a second.

I was becoming her safe place again. No chance in hell I'd jeopardize that.

Helping her into leggings and a sweater, I told her a little about our new home. It was closer to the playground. No one smoked indoors. Our roommate had cool drawings on his arms. No one yelled all the time. No Glenn.

Aunt Chrissy banged on the door, and I snapped. I stood up, opened the door, and pushed her up against the wall across the hall. Holy fuck, I was fuming.

"Show some motherfucking respect," I seethed. Her eyes grew large. "For a whole goddamn year, I've hated having Thea with you, knowing you scare her every fucking time you yell, throw something, smoke and drink in her presence, and don't give a shit about her boundaries. But I haven't had any choice—until now." I let go of her, disgusted and more than ready to leave.

We were done here.

———

Teach had offered to get us, but he was already doing so much. With my girl on my hip and her face buried against my neck, I shouldered the two duffels and picked up the garbage bag, and then we left Aunt Chrissy's building.

By the time we reached Olympia Square, the circulation was all but cut off in my arm, and I had to rest a minute. I didn't let go of Thea, but I dumped our shit on the ground.

"Daddy's outta shape." I scratched my hair through my beanie, sweaty. I hated sweating in the cold.

Thea gently tapped my cheek with her finger. Acknowledgment of what I'd said, I was pretty sure.

My phone beeped in my pocket, so I brought it out, my forehead creasing.

Can we meet?

It was from the guy who'd wanted to call me Martin.

I couldn't lie. It was tempting as fuck. Money was money.

I punched in a quick reply.

I quit doing that. If something changes, I'll let you know. You can delete this number.

That felt weird. It put a smile on my face I couldn't understand, but there was a heavy crush of guilt, too. I'd just turned down an easy seventy-five bucks.

After my break, Thea and I continued across the square

with our belongings. We reached Adrian's street, and he buzzed us in. He had an elevator in his building, which was a fucking relief today.

We rode up to the third floor, and the door to Teach's place was already open for us.

"Here we go, baby." I squatted down, a bit outta breath, and helped her off with her coveralls. "Are you ready to meet our new friend?"

She didn't answer, so I told her it was okay.

Adrian emerged from the hall where the two bedrooms were, and I was nervous. I had told him my girl didn't speak and that she had anxiety, so I expected questions about that later.

"Good morning, you two." He smiled and leaned casually against the wall. "There're bagels if you're hungry."

It smelled like freshly baked bread, so it wouldn't surprise me if he'd done them by himself.

"Thanks. Um, she's overwhelmed, I think." I stood up with Thea in my arms.

Adrian inclined his head. "Moving is a big deal. We can say hi when she's ready." His words meant a lot to me. A weight off my shoulders. He was making an effort to make her feel comfortable, something not even my aunt had done. "You told me Miss Thea likes to draw, yes?"

"She does." I kissed Thea on the forehead. "Ain't that right, baby?"

He nodded at the bedrooms. "Well, follow me, then." He grabbed the garbage bag, and I followed with the rest of the stuff.

The first bedroom down the hall was his, and then there was the bathroom on the other side. Adrian opened the final door, gesturing for us to go in first.

I'd expected to see the same guest room he had shown me last night. The bed was still in the corner, the white walls were still mostly bare, and the closet was still there, of course. But someone had been busy. He'd added a nightstand, put up a few shelves on the walls, and most of all, he had prepared a corner for Thea, complete with a desk, chair, and a few plastic boxes on the floor for toys. All this stood on a pink rug, and it was easier to go with a joke than get mushy.

"Should I worry that you keep pink rugs around?" I asked.

He grinned wryly. "Had it in the storage room. Unfortunately, it's the only thing left from my mother's collection of girly items. She always wanted a daughter."

"And she ended up with three boys," I said with a smirk.

"Poor woman." He chuckled. "When my folks sold their house, some of their things ended up in my storage unit. I wish there had been anything that was actually useful aside from this."

I shook my head and walked farther into the room. "It's perfect, Teach. Seriously."

Thea and I had never had this much. She'd had her own room at Aunt Chrissy's, but it'd been empty, except for her bed. She'd done her drawing on the floor or in the living room.

"Do you see this, Thea?" I murmured. Sitting down at the desk with her in my lap, I straightened the rubber mat on the desktop. "Adrian did it for you. You can draw and..." I trailed off when I opened the two drawers. "Damn."

Even Thea perked up. The drawers were full of pens, crayons, watercolors, and paper.

I swiveled the chair to thank Adrian again, but he wasn't there.

Thea tapped my neck with her finger, so I gave her my attention. There was no indication that she wanted to communicate, but when I asked if she wanted to explore her new place, she nodded quickly.

I didn't wanna leave her alone yet, so I began unpacking our things.

"Thea?" After about twenty minutes, I had absolutely nothing to do. I wanted to talk to Adrian. "I'm just gonna go out to the living room, okay? You wanna come with or stay here?"

She cocked her head and thought about it as she put down a crayon. Then she looked up at me and waved.

I couldn't help but laugh. "Is that a see-ya-later?"

She grinned and returned to coloring.

Fair enough. I left the door open and found Teach in the kitchen.

"Hey." I stuck my hands down in my pockets.

"Hey, there." He pulled a pan of bread from the oven. "Did you get settled in?"

I nodded. "I wanna thank you, for everything. You have no idea..." I rubbed the back of my neck. I was blank. Dazed. "It hasn't sunk in yet."

He smiled and hung up the oven mitts. "I'm glad I can help. How's Thea handling it? She's precious."

"I don't know. At this rate, you might become her favorite." I snorted and leaned against the counter. "She's stuck in her head, processing. The coloring stuff helps her."

"It pays being a teacher sometimes. Even if it's in markers instead of money." He winked at me. "Come here. You can help me divide these rolls into bags of six." He placed a roll of plastic bags next to the counter, which was full of bagels and cheesy rolls. "I'm taking it down to the Quad tomorrow before work."

So those who volunteered there made the food they served? That was generous. Or, I guessed...they volunteered what they could, be it in time or meals, and Adrian was an overachiever with a bleeding heart.

As I began putting six pieces of bread in each bag, he launched into a story about a project they were planning for the spring. I watched him. He spoke passionately about some of the kids who came to the Quad 'cause they had shitty families or whatever, and it was clear to me now that he was like Billy.

Bet, I'd been fucked over a lot, but I couldn't deny what happened right before my eyes. The events that had inspired Teach to do this shit were keeping him permanently fueled to make a difference. More than that, it was easy to see he enjoyed it.

"Tell me if I'm boring you," he said, amused.

I shook my head. "No. I was just thinkin'... You make Camas a pretty cool place to live."

His mouth quirked up in a lazy grin. "Good. I like this neighborhood, too. Not many do."

Yeah, I wasn't deaf. Whenever I was at the store or just around people here in general, there was a lot of bitching about Camas. I'd learned a little about the five 'hoods. Ponderosa in the north, where the loaded fuckers lived in hillside mansions. Westslope, which was mostly forests and mountain ranges, and for cabin owners and hunters. Downtown, the tourist hot spot and original town center. Supposedly, that part of Camassia Cove looked like a postcard for coastal towns. Then Cedar Valley, south of Camas, which was a trendy, newer district where the state college was. And basically, everyone talked smack about Camas.

Calling it a ghetto was fucking ridiculous, but what irritated me was the blatant disregard for those like Teach, who probably helped more citizens in a month than others did in their lifetimes. Privileged motherfuckers.

Okay, maybe I was getting heated about that topic. Whatever. It was true.

"Anything else I can do?" I was done with the dividing, and
I'd sealed the bags.

"Yes." He leveled me with a mock-serious look and gripped
my shoulders. I didn't tense up much this time. "Make yourself
at home."

I stared. He was being funny, I knew that. But his face... I
hadn't thought about his appearance before. Unless I counted
the times I'd assessed him to see if he posed a threat.

Now I saw more. Goddamn him. Fuck his kind eyes. Fuck
him for making it so difficult for me to keep my guard up. I'd
preached to myself all night about staying alert, and then I
looked at him...

For a fraction of a second, my gaze flitted to his mouth, and
then I quickly looked away, rattled as fuck. Why the hell had I
done that?

Jesus fucking Christ, was I living in my head today. I shook
it, annoyed.

Make myself at home, he'd said. I, uh...I could try, I
supposed.

7

The following week, I found myself standing outside Camas High. It was past lunch time, so Teach was probably in class. But I was too tempted to see him in action, so I went inside.

Willow would have Thea another hour. I had time.

A grouchy old bird outside the faculty lounge told me where I could find a Mr. Adrian Dalton, and I jogged up the stairs to the second floor where he had his classroom.

I grinned when I saw him through the window in the door. I was getting used to seeing him in jeans and sweats and beaters, most of his ink on display, but Teach was a teacher here. Jeans, button-down, tie, glasses. No tattoos visible whatsoever.

He was half sitting on his desk, arms folded over his chest, and discussing something with a room full of high school kids. If I listened closely, I could hear bits and pieces.

Teach chuckled at whatever a student had said, then nodded and absently tapped a whiteboard pen to his beard. "What do the rest of you think? Are we facing another revolution?" A girl raised her hand. "Ms. Diaz."

"Considering how we turn everything into an apocalypse today, there's always something called a revolution."

Several kids groaned, and someone complained that the girl was always overanalyzing crap and nitpicking on semantics.

"Simmer down, everyone." Teach rounded his desk and uncapped his pen to scribble on the board. "Ms. Diaz has a point, and it brings us to the homework you love so much. You can pair up."

I smirked as the students complained again. There was a chorus of "But, Mr. D!" ringing out. They obeyed fairly quickly, though.

In the meantime, Teach was listing a handful of *real* revolutions throughout history on the whiteboard. "We'll have a debate next week." I squinted to see what he was writing in another column. Modern *happenings* often referred to as revolutions. They weren't really revolutionary. "Okay, so here's what you're going to do..."

I shook my head and took a step back. I'd gotten sucked in too fast. Turning around, I walked through the empty hall and down the stairs. Adrian was a teacher who made school interesting. Or maybe it was just me. *And his class.* Hmm. The man gave me a mindfuck and didn't even know it.

When I came home—*I have a home*—Willow and Thea distracted me from my confusing thoughts about Adrian.

Every day, it became more evident that our move had been a good one. I'd been superfocused on money, how Aunt Chrissy had always wanted more money. It had kept dragging us down. But there was a fuckload more to it. Thea was coming to life. She wasn't acknowledging Adrian yet, aside from a few shy smiles, but that was temporary. She was more comfortable around him than she'd been after a year with Glenn.

She was a vibrant little thing, and that shit warmed my heart. She didn't hide. Didn't avert her gaze and try to blend in with the furniture as much. And when Adrian played music on the stereo, she came rushing out of our room to listen and bob her head.

Music was the focus today, I was informed. Willow scribbled her heart out and told me listening to music could ease Thea into making sounds on purpose. Lyrics could follow. Words. Step by step, the block that made my daughter clam up and go into full-on panic mode at the idea of speaking could crumble a bit.

"That's great news." I nodded, remembering I'd read an article about something similar in one of the textbooks I'd borrowed from Willow.

I was warned it could take years; Willow hadn't begun speaking to people she was comfortable around until she was eight or nine, and I waved that off. I was in no rush. I'd do my best to encourage it, obviously, 'cause being more high-functioning would improve Thea's situation as she grew up.

"Oh, by the way—" Willow froze at her own words, and fuck, so did I. Then she blushed and looked down while I was grinning ear to ear. I supposed that meant she was getting comfortable around me, if she was talking.

Thea paid no attention. She was having fun finding flash cards of ASL signs for me to learn. Giving Daddy homework was hilarious.

"It's okay, hon," I told Willow. "You don't gotta speak. We'll move on. You was saying something earlier about a playgroup?"

She nodded, avoiding eye contact. I didn't want her to be uncomfortable, though, I had to admit it was interested to see how Thea might react one day. I suspected it threw Willow off to go from being guarded...and then her brain decided it was okay to relax...? As if there were some disconnect and she couldn't control certain things.

Either way, we dropped the topic. Willow gave me a pamphlet about a program for special-needs kids in Ponderosa. When I could afford it, I'd be the first to look into it, since it didn't take a genius to figure out Thea needed to interact with kids her age.

As it was, she had fun with others on the playground, until they either thought she was weird for not talking, or until she determined they weren't having fun the right way. My girl could be a bossy little shit.

Before Willow left, she dug out a DVD from her bag. It was an educational cartoon for learning sign language, and there was dancing and music involved. Thea was so excited she could barely contain herself.

I was...going along with it.

We were at it for over an hour. I felt like an idiot, but Thea was having the time of her life. We followed the dance steps in front of the TV, mimicked the signs, and gave each other high fives for completing the routines.

I dropped a beat and rapped for her for a minute, too. She laughed like mad, eyes lighting up, which made me wonder if she remembered we used to do this all the time before.

That was how Adrian found us when he came home from work.

Not wanting him to see me making a fool of myself, I slumped down in his chair a sweaty mess.

Thea grunted as she tried to pull me up from my seat.

I chuckled and wiped my forehead. "Lemme rest, gangsta."

She huffed.

Adrian smirked and placed his briefcase on the table between the kitchen and living room. Since we'd moved in, I'd never seen the surface of that table. It was always filled with papers.

"Don't let me interrupt," he said. "In fact...Thea, will you teach me later? I want to learn your language, too." He gestured at the TV.

She nodded shyly and wrung her hands.

I smiled, unable to look away from him. Was I... What was it? Why did I stare at him so much? Was it just 'cause he was a considerate man?

My smile turned into a frown. He was still fucking with my head. I wasn't into overanalyzing.

Adrian winked at Thea and loosened his tie. "Perfect. Are you guys hungry?"

"I'll help." I stood up. "You wanna keep dancing, or should I turn off the DVD?" I looked down to Thea.

She went back to dancing and shaking her butt.

I joined Adrian in the kitchen, and it didn't take him long to ask how today's "errands" had gone. I thought about fucking with him but decided against it.

"It went fine, ya nervous Nellie." I smirked and folded my arms. "I'll get the negative results after the weekend."

The other day, he had not-so-subtly told me about his doctor buddy who ran his own practice. I'd walked down there today to get tested. Again.

"I'm glad you're confident." He opened the fridge and pulled out a plate with salmon. He'd gutted the fucking thing last night.

"I saw you afterward," I mentioned. "I got lost for a couple blocks on the way home and ended up outside Camas High."

"Yeah?" He got an expression of curiosity, so I told him I'd listened in on his class. When I said he seemed like a teacher kids listened to and respected, he was torn between proud and bashful.

Thea joined us in the kitchen with a note then, and I chuckled at her question written on it. "Can you rap again?" it said.

Adrian raised his brows. "Oh, I wouldn't want to miss this."

"How about later?" I suggested.

"No, now sounds good." Adrian smirked while Thea flashed me the puppy-dog eyes.

I shot him a scowl. I wasn't very good, and it was embarrassing in front of him.

Thea tugged on my hand and signed "Please."

Fuck.

I sighed in defeat and scratched my eyebrow. Then I got down on one knee next to her. "Aight, but you gotta help me." It was an opportunity to encourage her to make noises. "Ready?"

She nodded giddily and cupped her mouth with her hands like I'd done earlier.

Mirroring her pose, I started off with a slow beat, mimicking a kick-drum. We got into a rhythm, and she swayed with me. When she began making little *pshh-pshh* sounds, my day was made.

"Have you seen a li'l broad named Thea, she's a bit shy." I threw in some turntable effects that made her beam. "She's got these gorgeous peepers, she's about—yay high?" I lifted my hand to her height and imitated a hi-hat. "Yo, don't be confused. She's smart as hell, my little vice president—" We grinned and fist-bumped. "She'll school ya, fool ya, and welcome ya, to the fifth fuckin' element."

Thea squealed and clapped her hands, and then she mimicked a mic drop that made me laugh.

I'd been a jerk. Who cared if I goofed around like a fool? My girl was happy. It was all that mattered.

As I stood up, I caught Adrian smiling to himself while he put bits of salmon in a pan on the stove. Thea ran back to the living room, so I couldn't use her as a distraction.

"You were born to be her father, Dominic."

Shit.

My ears felt hot. "Thank you. Um, what can I do?"

He could undoubtedly sense I was uncomfortable with praise, so he switched topics. "I was meaning to ask you, actually. Did Dr. Stein say anything else? Did you talk?"

I narrowed my eyes. "That's a specific fucking question, Teach."

Yeah, his doctor buddy and I had spoken a bit. Mostly about safety and statistics, but he'd given me some pamphlets on "discovering your sexuality" and "recovering from bad experiences" and "remember, we are here." I thought it had looked like standard shit they gave out to those coming of age. I wasn't one of them, so I'd thrown 'em out.

"I may have hinted a little." Teach added more butter and asparagus to the pan. "You told me something that worried me, so I asked him if he could provide information on sexual trauma and—"

"*Dude.*" I widened my arms, offended as fuck. "Sexual trauma? You be buggin', man. I haven't been traumatized for shit."

He threw me an incredulous look. "You told me sex wasn't sexual. You wouldn't hesitate to suck me off, but you get paralyzed if I hug you. That, my friend, is fucking trauma." He paused as he checked the baby potatoes in the oven, and I gritted my teeth. I was conflicted. "I apologize for not discussing this with you earlier, but... No. To hell with it. Look me in the eye and tell me you would've gone to the doctor if I'd mentioned this sooner."

I couldn't do that. "You had no right."

"I took it."

What the fuck? Now I was pissed, and I flinched toward him. "Why?" I growled.

He didn't back down. "Because I give a shit," he snapped. Rather than giving me space, he walked closer and glared at me. "I fucking care, Dominic."

"I'm not your dead friend. You have no reason to care about me. We ain't blood."

Teach winced at the mention of his friend, and he looked down at the floor. I felt bad for a second, but I was fucking serious. Saving me wouldn't bring her back. Besides, he'd work himself into an early grave if he saw her in every person who lived destructively.

"I don't need a reason, and you of all people should know blood has very little to do with giving a rat's ass." He spoke with finality, refocusing on cooking as if I believed his charade. As if he wasn't cursing himself for letting me move in when he chopped the herbs with way too much force.

Shit. I'd fucked up.

He'd been wrong to go behind my back to basically tell the doctor I was some victim, but Jesus Christ. Why did I have to focus on that rather than seeing he was being a buddy and looking out for me?

I didn't know how to deal with this. I'd never been anyone's concern. At least, not since Mom died.

I swallowed my panic at the thought of going back to Aunt Chrissy. Oh, God. Back on the street. Would Adrian still let me sleep in his car?

"If you want me to move out, I get it, but if you could—"

"What?" He did a double take and frowned. "Don't be ridiculous. You're not going anywhere."

The relief hit me squarely in the chest, and I leaned back against the counter. God, I was almost shaking.

"Th-thanks," I muttered.

"No trauma, my ass." He abandoned the stove and approached me, placing his hands on my shoulders. "Look at me."

"How about fuck no?" 'Cause my vision was blurry, so *no*.

"All right. Don't freeze up; I'm going to hug you." There was a pinch of mirth in his voice, and then he wrapped me up in a tight hug.

I didn't go rigid and close up. If anything, it felt like a bomb went off inside me and something was released. Or unleashed. I shuddered as he stroked my back firmly. It felt *good*. Mad good. He smelled good, too. And he was always warm. Solid. Too fucking kind.

I circled my arms around his middle. It was awkward; it was so new, but I liked it. A lot. And in my head, I kept repeating the word *good*—how good it felt—but it was *more*. On another level. I wanted something. I hugged him harder, my forehead resting on his shoulder, and...I sounded like a goddamn broken record now, but it felt good. So good.

I understood him, too. His intentions.

"This...trauma, whatever-the-fuck you wanna call it," I said quietly. "It's not about what I've done to make money."

"Okay," he replied slowly. "Can we talk about it?"

I had no desire to do that whatsoever, but I owed him. "I guess. But our dinner's about to burn..."

"Fuck." Teach was overusing the F word today. He ended the hug, leaving me oddly bereft, and checked on the food. "Well, you can talk while I save this mess."

Of course he wouldn't postpone it or forget.

I sighed and racked my brain for what to tell him. "Um. There isn't much to say. I've been on my own a lot since I was a kid. Where I come from, not many people are kind for no reason. They want something in return." I rubbed the back of my neck. "You said I was in survival mode, and I guess that's true. It's a behavior. You can't show weakness, you know? It'll fuck you over fast. Same with depending on others. That won't work when you're out there on the street."

He was nodding along at that.

"So yeah, it's made me wary, and trust don't come easy."

"I understand. I can't imagine how difficult it's been, but..." He shook his head and brought out three plates. "Have you been able to rely on anyone at all? You've told me about Billy. I would've liked to meet him."

I lifted one shoulder. "My mom, I guess. She never won any Mom of the Year awards, but she was there."

Teach wavered. "What about Thea's mother?"

That made me snort. "If she's alive, she's got a needle stuck in her vein somewhere. We wasn't together or nothin'." I'd been thinking with my dick, and she thought she could get me starry-eyed enough to give her money. Several years older than me, she'd certainly made an impression; she was good in the sack. But I'd been closed off, only there to get my cock wet. "When she dropped the bomb and said I'd knocked her up, we agreed an abortion was best, but she bailed on me. Didn't see her for months, and then it was too late."

She'd had a habit of getting with anyone who could give her drugs.

"I got attached," I admitted. "I was infuriated and sure my life was over, but yeah, I got attached to the baby."

She hadn't. She'd been quick to sign over custody and disappear after giving birth.

"Sometimes, I wonder how you're still standing, Dominic. I can only admire you."

When he did that, said shit like that, I got uncomfortable. I could acknowledge that I was mentally strong. It took a great amount of effort to stand up after being knocked down repeatedly, but in the ways that mattered to me, I hadn't succeeded with anything other than surviving. I hadn't *lived* yet. I hadn't given my girl what she deserved.

"When did you start exchanging sex for money?" he asked.

I thought back. Had to have been shortly after we arrived in Philly. In New York, wherever we lived, I'd managed with gigs where I got paid under the table. Other than a brief stint as a no-good, street-corner hustler selling weed and ecstasy when I was sixteen, I had been on the right side of the law.

"About three years ago. After Thea was born," I answered.

Teach hummed, checking on the potatoes again. "I have your comment about sex not being sexual on my mind. I can understand doing what you did...you had to separate things. But before then, you never felt any attraction toward anyone?"

Attraction.

That word slapped me in the fucking face.

Oh God, I'd been stupid. I stared down at the floor, eyes wide. How hadn't that come to me sooner? It was *attraction.* That was the goddamn word I'd been looking for to describe what I felt.

I was attracted to this motherfucker.

"The reason I ask," Teach went on, oblivious to my inner chaos, "is that I'm curious if you've heard of asexuality."

Well, that worked. I snapped out it, if only for a moment, and cocked a brow. "Dude, I ain't asexual. My dick works just fine."

Admittedly, I didn't get turned on *often*, but...

"Shows how much you know about that," he muttered. "Asexuals aren't necessarily immune to physical stimuli. It's about attraction. For instance, a man watches porn and becomes aroused. Or he meets someone who turns him on. That's attraction, and if you're asexual, attraction is tricky. Nonexistent in many cases."

Huh. But considering the mother of aha moments I had seconds ago, I couldn't fall into that category. I just didn't know how far it went. I could admit that when I got hard, it wasn't at the thought of people. It was situational and about sensations.

It was difficult to picture doing anything sexual with Adrian for the sake of enjoying it, but on the other hand... If I took a shower now, I knew I'd be able to close my eyes and imagine breath on my neck, hands on my skin, and a wet mouth trailing down. All that would belong to him.

Was it possible to be attracted to the fantasy of being with him but not actually being *with* him?

8

For a whole week, the word "attraction" played on a loop in my head. I was becoming Adrian's personal peeping Tom 'cause I stared at him so much. As if he was a puzzle, and if I only looked at him a bit more, I'd understand.

It bled into my dreams, and one night fucked me up.

One second, Adrian and I were standing naked in front of each other. Gentle touches and warm kisses. No sudden movements. The next, he was giving it to me hard from behind and calling me a slut. It was twisted, leaving me both turned on and nauseated.

I woke up the next morning feeling like absolute shit, but it wasn't because of the vivid dreams. I was freezing, and my head weighed a ton.

Why did single parents get sick? We didn't have time for that.

Dragging my ass outta bed, I took a piss and washed up before tracking down Thea. It was early, and Adrian hadn't left for work. He was on the phone with someone in the kitchen, so I decided to get my girl dressed before making her breakfast.

The two things that stuck with me from the dreams were

kissing and him calling me a fucking slut. One of those was appealing, 'cause I'd never done it before. The other, no thanks.

"Come on, baby," I said hoarsely, finding Thea in the living room. "Big day for you."

"Willow," she mouthed.

I nodded. "That's right. You're going to the marina with Willow today."

I had a day of job hunting ahead of me.

In an attempt to push aside my confusion regarding Adrian, I had called it an early night yesterday. Then I had circled all the job ads in the *Camassia Courier* I could imagine I had at least a snowball's chance in hell of landing. Many of the places were in Cedar Valley, so it was time to buy a bus pass. So far, I'd been careful with Adrian's money, only buying some things for Thea and paying for babysitting.

As I was helping her into her clothes, she touched my cheek and had a look of concern. Too fucking cute.

"I'm fine," I assured her, only to get caught in a dizzy spell when I stood up. "Damn." I shook my head and grabbed her hairbrush. "Straighten out that bedhead, gangsta. I'mma fix your breakfast."

I joined Adrian in the kitchen and made as little noise as possible. He was speaking to someone at the same time as he fixed his tie and waited for his toast to pop up.

Grabbing the last of Thea's yogurts, I stole furtive peeks at Adrian's mouth and did my best to look busy. I poured a glass of milk, then sliced a banana.

If I concentrated hard, I could almost slow down time in my head. He nodded at whatever and wet his bottom lip.

What would it be like to kiss? What would it be like to kiss *him*? His lips looked soft, yet firm. The other day, he'd trimmed his beard, too. I liked it.

What I didn't like was the idea of him calling me slut.

"Thank you, Mike, I appreciate it." He was wrapping up the call. "Definitely, and he'll be there."

I added the banana to the yogurt and added both items to the grocery list on the fridge. Thea was sensitive to dairy products, and since she was obsessed with cheese, I bought milk and yogurt that were free of lactose.

"Good morning." Adrian pocketed his phone and smiled, but it faded when he looked at me. "You don't look well. How are you feeling?"

I shrugged and got out of the way so he could get the butter for his toast.

"Hmm." He came closer and lifted his hand. It covered my forehead, and I shivered at the cold. "Christ, you're burning up."

"No, you're cold as fuck. Whatta you, some fucking vampire now?"

That smile he smiled, the lazy one where one of the corners of his mouth twisted up more than the other—I liked that one. Then he got serious again. "You're staying home today. Rest."

I snorted. "I don't think so, Pop. I gotta find a job."

"What if I just found one for you?" he challenged.

"Did you?" I asked, surprised.

He inclined his head and resumed fixing his breakfast. "It's only three nights a week, but it's a start." He crammed half a slice of bread into his mouth. "You'll be cleaning a bar after closing." As he licked butter off his thumb, he used his free hand to scribble down a number and an address on a note. "Monday at three PM, ask for Mike."

I stared at the note, a grin spreading across my face. My first legit job. "Are you fucking with me?"

He shook his head and then smiled down at something behind me. "Morning, angel. Don't you look beautiful?"

I turned to see that Thea had put approximately two dozen

hair clips in her curly mess. She grinned crookedly and waved hello.

"You're a nut," I chuckled. Which hurt. Goddamn, I was getting worse. "Time to eat. Go sit down." I followed her with her breakfast, and as she got to eating, I put on cartoons for her. Then I dipped down and kissed her on the forehead. "Prettiest girl in the world. I'll be back, just gotta take a shower."

She nodded.

I headed for the bathroom and pulled off my T-shirt on the way. Once there, I almost bumped into Adrian, who'd just brushed his teeth.

"Stay home today," he said and wiped his mouth. "I'll make my famous chicken soup tonight. Thea should like it, too."

I hesitated. It was Thursday, so he would already be home late since he volunteered at the Quad.

"I need to pitch in more."

At that, he gave me his full attention. Hands on my shoulders, that serious "I'm a teacher; I know what I'm talking about" expression.

"Can't you let someone take care of you for once?" he asked. "You're sick."

Teachers liked to talk. He went on to lecture about being careful and listening to what your body was telling you. And wasn't that a kick in the head? Sure, my body was telling me to rest and go easy today, but that wasn't all. I *heard* him. I didn't *listen*.

His mouth formed the words I was supposed to consider.

I licked my lips.

If I only leaned in a little...

Damn.

Before I knew what I was doing, I shut him up by leaning forward and brushing my mouth to his. That ghosting touch had the same effect my aha moment had last week. My heart kicked into overdrive, and my pulse skyrocketed.

Adrian stood stock-still.

I kissed him again, longer. Slowly. More pressure. I was right. His lips were soft but still firm. His breath—fuck. Minty. Fresh. Shallow puffs of air hit my lips, and I had to taste. I closed my eyes.

The moment the tip of my tongue carefully swiped across his bottom lip, he let out a quiet groan that shook me up. I shuddered, and then he was kissing me back. He took charge, 'cause I was inexperienced like nothing else, but he kept it slow. Seductive as fuck.

Testing the waters, I cautiously cupped his jaw. Under the raspy beard was a chiseled jaw that moved with each kiss. It was heady. I'd had no fucking clue. He tasted delicious and felt so good. It was comforting and thrilling all at once. I'd never experienced that thrill.

It sent bursts of heat through me, leaving me flushed and shaky.

His hands came to my hips, and he deepened the kiss. Tasting him on his tongue, wet and sensual and warm and sliding along mine, was outta this fucking world. I moaned and pressed myself harder against his body.

"Fuck," he whispered.

I found myself caught between him and a wall. A ball of nerves rose within me, but it was silenced. *I* silenced it. I didn't want this to be over. Kissing was a new favorite. Holy fuck, it was *amazing*.

"Adrian..." I trembled and stroked his neck with my fingers, angling my head to go deeper.

"Oh, God—" He gave me another fierce, body-melting kiss before he slowed down and eventually broke away.

I was panting. I hadn't realized. He opened his eyes, and I was trapped. I wondered if mine looked as wild as his.

"Why did you do that?" he whispered roughly.

I swallowed dryly, tasting him everywhere. "I don't know." Because I fucking had to. I had to know, and now I knew, and I was going insane.

As the heavy fog of crazed lust lifted, the pain was back. My head was killing me. I wanted him to take it away with more kissing. As if to prove a point, my gaze dropped to his mouth. I knew what those lips felt like now. I knew what they tasted like and how he'd made me forget the goddamn world.

I'd heard the phrase "making out like teenagers." If I hadn't fucked shit up by coming on to him, we had to try that.

"Next time—" he swallowed "—you better know why."

Next time.

He left the bathroom, adjusting himself, a sight that made me more aware of things. Had I made him hard? Looking down, I grabbed my crotch and felt it was pretty hard, too. Goddamn.

I shuddered.

The minute I got better, I wanted to kiss him again.

I touched my lips and grinned.

First kiss: check.

Thoughts of kissing disappeared. Willow had come for Thea, Adrian had left for work, and my body grew heavier and heavier. In the end, I collapsed on the couch. I'd snatched up both my duvet and Adrian's, but I was still freezing.

The dizziness and the headache made me sick to my stomach too, though I never had to hurl. Silver lining, I supposed. Instead, I slept restlessly all fucking day.

Willow called late in the afternoon and asked if she could

bring Thea home for dinner with her grandmother. I mumbled, all but incoherent to my own ears, that it was fine, and then I returned to sleep.

At some point, it got hot. My dreams held me captive. They were a fucked-up, twisted mess, kind of like last night. Sinister met sweet, rough against gentle, evil versus kind. My gut churned. It got hotter and hotter, and sweat was pouring from me.

Adrian's hands were on me. He held me down. I couldn't see his eyes. He wouldn't look at me as he fucked me into a mattress of concrete. When he was done, he threw a few bills next to me and left.

I clutched my stomach and groaned in pain.

I swam through a haze, lost until I saw shadows.

A better, kinder, realer version of Adrian appeared in my dreams. My muscles unclenched as he kissed my forehead and removed whatever it was that had pushed me down. I felt lighter. He murmured things to me; I couldn't hear, and I didn't care. The heat wasn't as bad anymore. There was even a breeze.

He brushed away sweat-dampened hair from my forehead and stroked my cheek. I leaned into him and mumbled that he was my favorite Adrian.

He chuckled quietly, and then he disappeared, only to return with a glass of water and two painkillers. Another layer was also taken off me before he fanned out simple sheets over my body. It felt nice.

This Adrian had the teacher voice, too. He told me gently to take the painkillers, and he even held my head because it was so fucking heavy. The water was cold, and I moaned at how good it tasted. I hadn't realized I was parched.

I wanted to cuddle him, and I told him as much, though I was too weak to lift a finger.

He said I was funny.

Feeling slightly better, I shrugged and stretched out. I told him I'd never cuddled before, not counting Thea, so who could blame me for trying? I yawned and tried to open my eyes, but that was a no-go. I was too tired. The concrete mattress was gone, leaving me comfortable on a couch instead.

It was perfect, I made sure to mention. Almost as perfect as my first kiss earlier.

Something smelled good.

Cracking my eyes open took more strength than it should, and my head was fucking pounding, but at least I felt better than before. I was disoriented, my mouth dry, and I had little control over my body. But something had to give, 'cause I needed to piss.

I hauled myself off the couch with a groan and scrubbed my hands over my face.

The apartment appeared empty, so I stumbled my way into the bathroom. I was lucid and in less pain. Vague memories reminded me I'd been sweating like an animal earlier. That should mean the fever was gone. I supposed I could count myself lucky it had only been a twenty-four-hour bug—not even that.

One glance in the mirror said I looked like shit. A shower was in order, especially since I'd never showered this morning.

I didn't linger long under the hot spray. I was too exhausted, but now I was clean and smelled of soap instead of sweat. Wrapping a towel around my waist, I exited the bathroom and shivered at the nip in the air.

The door leading to the fire escape was open in the living room, so I closed that shit.

"Dominic?"

"Holy fuck." I turned around, taken off guard, and saw Teach emerging from the bedroom hallway. "I didn't know you was home."

He barely glanced at me, maybe 'cause I was only wearing a towel. "Were."

"Seriously." I shot him a look.

He laughed and proceeded to go to the kitchen. "Sorry, couldn't help myself. Come on, you need to eat."

No argument from me. I followed him, confused when I passed the dining room table. There were even more tests and homework, not to mention a mug of steaming coffee and a bag of sweets. He'd been home a while.

"What fucking time is it?" I squinted.

"Almost ten."

"Uh, what?" I stiffened, worried. "Yo, Thea's not home yet—"

"Relax, sweetheart. I just put her to bed."

I opened my mouth, then clamped it shut again. Reaching for a chair that wasn't used as a bookshelf, I plopped down and stared. My mind was sluggish. I held up a finger, only to lower it again. For fuck's sake, I wasn't about to speak out loud.

But, *firstly*, I'd lost an entire day. I'd missed Thea coming home. Slept through it all.

Secondly, she must've lowered her guard around Adrian if she let him help her. That made me happy.

Thirdly, did Adrian call me sweetheart?

I rubbed my forehead, in the mood to bitch and whine. I was useless tonight. Hell, I hadn't even bothered to get dressed.

"You say the funniest things when you're sick," Adrian noted.

I frowned tiredly at him. He was making—or reheating—soup on the stove. "I'm exhausted and my head's momentarily retarded. I'm sure I've been a fucking comedian."

He hummed and rotated his shoulder, like it was sore. "I throw books at my students when they use the r-word."

I snorted a laugh. "Do you really?"

"No," he admitted. "In my mind, perhaps. Over and over."

Duly noted.

I grew quiet and slouched back in my seat, done thinking. I couldn't do it. Instead, I watched Teach prepare supper. Watching him improved my mood, too. He'd turned into my hobby. Some watched TV, I checked out my roommate.

We kissed this morning. It wasn't incomprehensible anymore. I just wanted to do it again and again and again. Maybe he'd woken me up. Whatever it was, I was starving for the kind of closeness I'd shied away from all my life.

Technically, it hadn't been a difficult job to avoid affection. There hadn't been many interested in closeness with me to begin with. Those who had—nah, motherfucker. Couldn't be trusted.

I remembered this one guy in Philly. For months, he texted me two or three times a week. He wanted the boyfriend experience. Like, he wanted us to snuggle and shit? He was always pushing for that. Kissing, holding hands. He'd creeped me the fuck out.

Now I could recognize he was probably lonely. I'd turned him down every time. I sucked him like a champ, and not surprisingly, guys who had their dicks trapped between a set of teeth rarely pushed their luck. But the idea—back then—to get close enough for someone to *hold* me...? I would've panicked and killed us both.

"How you doin'?" I jerked my chin at him. "You haven't felt sick today or anything?"

He shook his head, tossing a couple of rolls into the microwave. "My immune system could only be better if I worked with toddlers instead of teenagers. I rarely get sick." He paused, deliberating, then slid me a look of wry amusement. "But thank you for putting me at risk this morning."

I averted my gaze and rubbed the back of my neck. "Shit."

Adrian chuckled. "Don't worry about it. I wasn't exactly complaining."

Well, hell. Could we do it again, then? Now?

I was losing my mind.

Who knew kissing was glorious?

I was about to ask if we could revisit, but he declared supper was ready. He passed me on his way to the living room, a tray in his hands. I trailed after him like a dog 'cause I saw the bowls of soup, the buttered rolls, and glasses of milk. Fuck, I was hungry. I hadn't eaten anything all day.

"I hope you don't mind if I work while we eat," Teach said.

"No, of course not." I sat down on the couch and grabbed my bowl while he went to get some paperwork. As soon as he got seated next to me and the red pen came out, I deduced it was time to grade some tests.

I turned on the news, though I sure as fuck didn't pay attention.

"Christ, you're a god in the kitchen," I muttered. The chicken was torn into tiny bits, mixed with vegetables and chunks of potato. How I'd ever measure up, I had no idea.

"You're great for my ego." He smiled, slid on his glasses, and marked a paper with B+.

Dipping my bread into the soup, I side-eyed him as he worked. Now that I knew I was physically drawn to the fucker —attracted—I could admit watching him was sexy. *He* was sexy.

I became hyperaware of everything he did. He put down his pen to eat, though his gaze never strayed from the test. His mouth closed around the spoon, and his Adam's apple bobbed when he swallowed. Next, he tore off a bit of bread and was about to eat it, but he caught something on the test and forgot his supper.

I grinned.

I was nuts, I got it. Couldn't be helped, though. He continually amazed me with his dedication, devotion, and passion. Adrian was a smart guy. He looked good; he could be the guy you brought home to your parents, and he could be the fierce motherfucker you didn't mess with. Nonjudgmental, generous, skilled, and definitely humble.

"Why the fuck don't you have a man?" I blurted out. "I mean..."

I didn't get how he was single.

He lifted a brow, confused. "Pardon?"

"Look at'chu." I shrugged. "You got a good job, have your own place, you're hot... You're a good man. Why're you single?"

Adrian cleared his throat and laughed a little. If I didn't know any better, I'd say he took compliments as well as I did.

"Well, it's by choice. At the moment, anyway." He stalled by finishing his bread. "I was with my ex for two years, and we ended our relationship last summer."

Hmm. Maybe I shouldn't have asked. I didn't wanna hear about him with some other motherfucker. It didn't sit right with me.

"Casual sex isn't my scene, so..." He gestured at the tests. "I've focused on work."

"Do you miss him?" I asked and adjusted my towel. *Stupid.* What if he said yes?

"No." He shook his head. "We wanted different things, and when I couldn't meet him halfway, which he deserved, we decided it was best to break up and just be friends."

"Oh." I was strangely relieved he didn't miss his ex. "What different things?"

"We were living together in Downtown," he explained. "I

never liked it up there. Being part of this community has always mattered to me, so I wanted to live here in Camas. Whereas he wanted us to get a house in Ponderosa."

It showed what he thought about that. I almost laughed. "So I'll get to meet him one day?"

Adrian had told me he wanted to introduce me to some friends he went to a bar with sometimes. I wouldn't mind checking the dude out, for reasons I could only describe as irrational.

"I highly doubt that," he chuckled. "Shortly after our breakup, he accused me of moving on too fast. In a nutshell, he was pissed because I didn't mope around. It ended our friendship before it really began."

When he stifled a yawn, I felt bad. Not only was I keeping him from working, but he was tired.

"To hell with it." Teach removed his glasses and tossed them on the table before rubbing his eyes. "I can work tomorrow. I don't have any classes, so you'll be stuck with me all day."

There were worse things.

"Why don't you have classes?"

"Field trip." He leaned back, closed his eyes, and absently rubbed his shoulder. "Unless you have work next Thursday, mind coming down to the Quad with me? We're a few men short, and I had to break up two fights tonight."

What the fuck? "Yeah, of course. You shoulda called me down there today. I could've helped." I frowned at his shoulder. Had someone hurt him? "I didn't know shit gets rough down there."

I'd pictured kids playing pool or shooting the shit while adults supervised and offered support because the students' parents sucked.

"It's not often." He was dismissive about it. "A boy got cocky today, though. They're a bunch of hotheads, and if you don't show them who's in charge, they'll take advantage."

I was familiar with that mentality.

"Count me in," I said firmly. "I can call Willow so I can be there more than Thursdays."

Adrian lolled his head along the backrest and cracked a sleepy smirk at me. "I appreciate it, but it's okay. We're really only understaffed on Thursdays and Fridays."

I shrugged. "Aight, so I'll be there then until I can't 'cause of work."

It was about time I saw what he was doing down there, anyway. Besides, it mattered to him, and he'd done so much for me. Time for me to give something back.

"Want me to rub your shoulder?" I offered. "I give good massages." Complete bullshit, but how hard could it be?

"You don't have to do that."

No, but I wanted to help. And get my hands on him. "I know." I crammed the last of my roll into my mouth and twirled a finger. "Turn around."

"Actually..." He leaned forward and looked reluctant to say whatever he was gonna say. "I should go to bed. It's been a long day."

Well, fuck. I bit the inside of my cheek, keeping my mouth shut. Adrian gathered his things, and I just sat there. My body was tired, but I wasn't sleepy. If I tried to go to bed now, I'd lie there and think too hard on everything and nothing. But Adrian was done for the day. More than that, I could tell he was escaping.

We exchanged goodnights, and then he disappeared down the hall. I guessed I'd been too focused on when he'd said "Next time." Now I wasn't sure what he meant by that, but I was beginning to doubt he was interested.

Making a lame-ass attempt at distracting myself, I rested my chin in my palm and watched TV. I didn't know what it was about. My foot tapped on the rug. My fingers drummed along my cheek. I kept glancing toward the hallway.

"Fuck this," I whispered. If he wasn't interested, I needed to know. Then I could move on and quit obsessing. Standing up, I tightened the towel around my hips and debated what to say.

Outside Teach's door, I lifted my arm to knock, only wavering for a beat or two.

It took a few seconds before I heard his voice. "Yeah?"

9

I opened the door, my mind still working out what I was gonna say.

Adrian sat up in his bed and hunched forward, and I recognized the look in his eyes. It was similar to this morning, I was fucking sure of it.

Fuck, fuck.

"Is something wrong?" There was a hint of impatience in his tone.

A ball of nerves tightened in my gut, 'cause it was goddamn clear I'd interrupted him jacking off.

"I, uh..." I swallowed. My legs carried me closer of their own volition as I eyed his exposed chest. His covers pooled around his middle, and I had to admit I wasn't too stoked about taking this too far. I didn't wanna get fucked, but...if he could agree to give more kissing a go, I could get through it. If he wanted.

"Dominic," he warned.

"Why're you saying it like that?" I stopped when my knees hit the bed, and I was frustrated. Frustrated 'cause I didn't understand what was going on with me or why I cared this much. "I can't stop thinking about this morning, so if you're not interested, you gotta tell me."

"*Fuck*." He looked away from me and scrubbed a hand down his face.

He *was* interested.

In a bold move, I got up on the bed, one knee between his thighs. His head whipped back, eyes fixed in a glare. In return, I cupped his face gently. He had time to push me away. As I stroked his skin, his beard, and brushed my thumb over his bottom lip, he had every opportunity to tell me to fuck off.

He didn't. Instead, he closed his eyes and leaned forward, resting his forehead on my chest. A shudder ripped through me when I felt his larger hands sliding up the backsides of my thighs. Under the towel.

I should've thought this through and put on sweats or some shit, but it was too late now. He wouldn't hurt me, I knew that, and if he wanted to fuck me, I was a pro at closing myself off.

Dipping down, I kissed the top of his head and lingered. I breathed him in and waited for him to tilt his face up. When he did, I wet my lips and captured his mouth with mine right away.

Fuck. Yeah.

I could get addicted to this.

This time, I wasn't as cautious. I wanted to taste him again, feel his tongue sliding along mine, so I applied pressure and nipped at his lip. He parted his lips and cursed, then deepened the kiss.

My stomach did a somersault as he fell back against the mattress and pulled me with him. A gasp escaped me. I was on top of him, so I didn't feel suffocated or trapped. This could work. Hell, this worked *perfectly*.

I cupped his cheek and groaned into his mouth. He was more careful. His hands stayed on my hips, and he let me lead.

I made him moan when I sucked on his tongue and stroked the soft skin along the shell of his ear.

"You sleep talk," he said, breaking away to kiss my neck. I wanted his mouth on mine again. "You told me..."

"What?" I sucked in a breath, registering the fact that he was hard as a fucking rock. And I wasn't panicking. It was that thrill again. It shot heat through my veins.

"You said I was your first kiss." He cupped the back of my neck and searched my eyes. "Was I?"

I nodded and kissed him once more. "More kissing, less talking."

He let out a breathy laugh but obeyed for a minute. Though, he wasn't done talking. When was a teacher ever?

"I'm afraid to hurt you, Dominic. Actually, I'm afraid I'll get hurt in the process, too."

I frowned, my hooded gaze refusing to leave his thoroughly kissed lips. "How are you gonna hurt me?"

I didn't ask how I'd hurt him, 'cause that was ridiculous. I'd never hurt him.

"By losing my head and taking advantage," he murmured. I hummed in acknowledgment and began kissing his neck and sternum. If he insisted on wasting time on words, I could have fun in the meantime. "You sitting in that fucking towel drove me crazy."

Oh.

"You hid it well." I licked the spot behind his ear before moving down to his chest. "God..." I eye-fucked him, feeling something stirring in my gut. It was lust. Sheer fucking lust. I tasted more. I licked and kissed his defined muscles. I grazed my teeth around his nipples.

Adrian hissed.

"What do you want?" I asked to get it over with.

He shook his head and pulled me closer again. "Don't ask

that." He kissed me hard and deep, pushing his tongue into my mouth.

I was in heaven. I got what I wanted, and we made out like teenagers. It made me lose track of time. My internal defenses were forgotten, something taking its place. A frenzy. I couldn't get enough.

Frustration built up. "I need...*something*," I growled. As if he knew what, he palmed my ass and pushed me down, grinding his crotch against mine, and it set me on fucking fire. I choked on the pleasure and nearly lost my shit. "Fuck! Oh, God..." I melted into another drugging kiss, and I moved with him. I couldn't describe the sensations.

My cock was hard, and it was all because I was feeling his. Needing just a bit more, I kicked off the thick duvet in between us. I never looked down, but I could tell he wasn't wearing anything.

It turned me on further, almost as much as his sexy groans.

"We need to stop," he gritted out.

"No, we really don't." I thrust forward and shuddered violently. I wasn't completely stupid; if I kept this up, I would blow my load on him. But it felt so good...

"We do." He gripped my hips hard, stilling me. He blew out a labored breath, looking almost pained. "I'm about two seconds away from begging you to fuck me, so yeah, we have to stop."

I blinked.

Asking *me*...to fuck...*him*...?

For the first time, I peered down. My towel was coming loose, and I ripped it away out of pure instinct. I had to see. Ignoring Adrian's hissed curse, I stared at his cock lined up with mine.

I touched him gingerly first, waiting for the moment to be ruined by my tainted past. It didn't happen. Maybe 'cause my body and mind were on the same page, for fucking once. There was no disconnect. I could trust Adrian. I could let myself be turned on. It was intimate, and sex was becoming sexual. Because it was him.

"I want to." I glanced at him as I stroked his cock slowly. We were almost the same in size, except he was longer. He wasn't cut like I was, and the skin that stretched around him was soft and smooth. I swallowed, my mouth watering. "I wanna fuck you."

It'd been ages—and with a broad—but I wasn't clueless about this, at least.

Teach clenched his jaw and rubbed his thumb over a scar on my bicep. "I won't be able to say no."

"Good."

I sat back on my heels between his parted legs, and he dug through his nightstand drawer for rubbers. And lube. Lube was a luxury. Much better than spit.

Adrian sat up and yanked me closer, and he kissed my lower abs as he fisted my cock. It startled me, a jolt of pleasure causing me to buck forward. I felt his breath on me, and then he rolled the condom down my dick in one stroke.

"Fuck, I want to suck you off," he muttered.

Another time.

I pushed him down again and took the bottle of lube. I coated my cock and gave it a couple quick strokes. "Um, fingers first?"

He shook his head. "Just your cock."

A bit nervous, I wiped my hand on my thigh. Then I leaned over him and positioned the head of my dick at his ass. I rubbed it over the hole, teasing him. He made a sound of frustration at that, which made me grin shakily.

I pushed in slowly, inch by inch. It was the hottest fucking thing. He was tight and all slicked up. Squeezing me. He spurred me on with gritty moans and filthy whispers about how he'd fantasized about my cock for weeks.

Overwhelmed like some pathetic virgin, I had to pause when I was all in.

"Jesus Christ, Dominic." He grabbed my face and kissed me hard. "Fuck me."

I groaned and pulled out, then pushed in. His hands were rougher on me now, but rather than triggering anything bad, it ignited me.

It didn't take long for me to lose myself in the moment again.

"Need it bad?" I asked huskily.

"God, yes." He shuddered when I wrapped my fingers around his cock. "Don't tease me."

"I won't." I dipped down and kissed him deeply. "I wanna give it to you." Pulled out. "Over..." Shoved my cock inside. "And over. And fucking over."

He groaned, meeting every thrust. His hands returned to my ass, and I loved how he dug his fingernails into my flesh and physically begged for more. I didn't need his words. I was getting off on his expressions instead.

"You like it," I whispered. "You like getting fucked hard."

"Yeah." He panted and sucked my bottom lip into his mouth. "Sometimes. Now."

"What else do you like?"

"A lot." His eyes flashed with dark desire. "I love sucking off a beautiful, thick cock like yours." *Shit.* I sped up, spellbound. "Just as I love waking up to a warm, wet mouth taking my cock deep and swallowing my come."

I licked my lips and looked down. I gave it to him harder, gritting my teeth as the muscles in my thighs throbbed.

"I love it hard, gentle, fast, and slow." He nuzzled my neck and nipped at my skin sharp enough to elicit a hiss from me. "Both as a top and a bottom."

"Fuck, Adrian..." I gasped. Squeezing my eyes shut, I began pounding into him. It was getting to be too much. My balls felt tight and full. Blood surged in my cock.

I stroked him fast. My gaze flicked between his cock, slick with pre-come, and his handsome face contorted in bliss, and... just, fuck, everywhere. I drank him in. Swallowed repeatedly. Images forming in my head. No longer as terrifying.

Rather than thinking "maybe one day," my mind settled on "hopefully, soon." I hoped to experience all that—everything he loved. I hoped to enjoy it as much as he did.

"You need to come," he bit out. "I'm close."

Thank fuck!

He took over stroking himself, and I got to watch him do it while I slammed in and out of him. His abs tensed. His thighs looked thicker with the strain. Unbelievably hot.

I loved his chest. The definition of his muscles, the tattoo covering one pec and slithering down to his ribcage, his smattering of soft chest hair.

"Oh—" The orgasm crashed down on me without much warning. I had the image of his forearms flexing as he jacked his cock etched in my brain. Eyes closed, I railed him hard one more time and then let go.

I groaned hoarsely, unable to move. My cock pulsed inside him, and his tight ass clenched down on me as I filled the condom. Only a moment later, hot splashes of come landed on our chests. The scent of sex invaded me and sent more tingling ecstasy through me.

"Fuck, fuck, fuck..." I panted. I didn't collapse on him completely. My forehead landed on his shoulder. I opened my eyes and saw the liquid on his chest, and I drew one finger through it.

He winced, as if sensitive or ticklish. "Spend the night with me."

I nodded and pulled out of him. "Yeah, can we cuddle?" I wanted closeness.

There was a grin in his voice. "Oh, I fucking insist."

"Cool." I smiled. The nerves were coming back, only 'cause I didn't know the protocol. "Um, can we shower? We're sticky."

I didn't like the mess. I'd go too far by calling it dirty, but it didn't offer any fond memories, either.

"Of course."

Minutes later, we were sharing the small space of his shower, Adrian was crazy affectionate. I basked in his warmth, the sweet but firm strokes of his hands on my body, his kisses, and I did my best to process everything.

I'd fucked Teach. I'd been the top.

"You have a lot of scars," he murmured.

I peered down at myself and lifted one shoulder. "It happens."

He cupped my face and kissed me softly. "You're fucking beautiful."

"Do you really think so?" I searched his eyes, and in my opinion, he was the beautiful one.

"Beautiful, sexy..." He gave my neck an openmouthed kiss. "Hot, edgy, handsome, gorgeous..."

I shuddered and wiped away water from my face. "I could say the same about you."

"Oh yes, I'm definitely edgy."

His warm chuckle made me smile, and he pressed a kiss to my forehead.

I squinted up at him. "So, I don't think I'm asexual."

He stared at me before bursting out a laugh. "No. No, I don't think so, either."

I woke up the next morning trapped under an arm and a muscular leg. Blinking drowsily, I saw the sun was filtering through the blinds of a window that wasn't positioned right. *Oh.* Because I wasn't in my room. Panic rose quickly before I remembered where I was and whose arm was holding me close.

Adrian.

"Off'a me," I grunted, lifting his heavy arm.

Maybe he was already awake, 'cause he moved away fast. "I'm sorry."

Much better. I sighed in contentment and rolled around to snuggle into his chest. "Mornin'."

He seemed careful. "Good morning." Slowly but surely, he drew me into his warmth and kissed the top of my head. "Are you all right?"

I nodded, my lips brushing against his chest. I was feeling great. Being held down didn't work for me, but this? This was heaven. "It's gotta be early if Thea's not up yet. Wanna make out?"

He shook with silent laughter. "As much as I would like that, I heard her a while ago. I believe she's watching TV."

"All right." I yawned and stretched out, feeling inspired. It was gonna be a good day, and I wanted to make the most of it. Since I was sick yesterday, today would be dedicated to job hunting in Cedar Valley. "I should go give Willow a call."

"Why?"

"I wanna head down to Cedar Valley and look for more work." I sat up and rubbed my eyes.

I needed to shave.

"You don't have call her, you know." Teach sat up too, and his feet hit the floor with a thud. "I'm working from home today. I'd be happy to look after Thea."

Reaching for my discarded towel, I stood up and wrapped that around me. I wasn't sure about him watching Thea. No doubt, he was capable. I knew he was great with kids by now. That said, I was done putting more on his shoulders.

He was becoming a big part of my life, whatever that meant. It'd hurt if he soon saw me as a burden.

"It's cool," I said, moving toward the door. "I'll call Willow. Don't worry about it." I flashed him a smile before ducking out into the hallway.

10

Life got busy for me over the next several weeks, and I fucking loved it. I'd actually managed to find a job on my own, too. Combined with the two gigs Teach had landed me, I was slowly working my way toward full-time employment.

Three nights a week, I cleaned a bar. Mike was a cool guy, old-school, and from the East Coast. He'd hooked me up with Diego, a dude who owned a Mexican restaurant on the same street as Mike's bar in Cedar Valley. I was a busboy there now, and he'd been generous with my schedule. Three shifts, on the same days I was at Mike's. So I worked at Diego's first and then went across the street to Mike's when his bar closed.

Last but not least, Teach had gotten me an interview at the grocery store in Camas. It was earlier this week I got the job, so now I was stocking shelves on Mondays and Tuesdays.

I hoped to have all my jobs in Camas at some point, so I wouldn't stop looking. The downside of living in a small town with shitty public transportation was that I had to walk home in the middle of the night.

Of course, Adrian had insisted on picking me up at first. He'd reminded me that this was Washington and wildlife wasn't a myth. But walking along the side of the road that crossed a small forest between the two districts didn't take more than ten minutes, and I hadn't seen so much as a fucking deer.

Besides, if he were to come get me, he'd have to wake up Thea, too.

Outta the question.

Learning to drive and getting my license were on the list, but I couldn't afford that shit right now. It would come later.

"Excuse me?"

"Huh?" I turned from the shelf of cereal I was restocking and saw an old lady pointing up.

"Do you mind, dear? I can't reach," she said.

I looked up toward what she wanted. "Yeah, sure." I grabbed a box of Lucky Charms and handed it to her.

She smiled. "Thank you. For the grandkids."

"Okay." I gave her a polite smile and then returned to unpacking boxes of Kellogg's. I wanted to finish quickly so I could take a break to call Mike about my schedule.

Last Thursday, Adrian had come home from the Quad with a fucking bruise along his ribs. They were having problems with a kid whose parents were losing everything, and he was lashing out. At Teach. The kid came to the Quad to get away, but he was acting like a dick to those who gave a shit.

If I could just get Mike to change my hours a bit, I'd finally be able to help Adrian at the Quad. That was weighing on me heavily. Between work and being there for Thea as much as possible, it wasn't easy to find time, but I had to. One way or another.

It often came back to Adrian. I wanted to do things for him all the time, not because I owed him, but because...I wanted.

Finished with the cereal, I cleared the aisle and headed out back to throw away the trash. Then I stepped outside and brought out my phone.

Spring in Washington was a joke. It was cold as fuck.

Mike answered on the fourth ring.

"You sure?" I asked.

Marla nodded. "Don't worry, it gets thrown away otherwise."

"Okay, thank you." I accepted the bag and peered inside it. It made me grin. There was a bunch of stuff—groceries that were expiring soon. Bread, eggs, fish, even a couple steaks.

Another employee came over, and Marla handed her a bag, too.

"Just don't tell Mr. Stick-up-his-ass." She winked.

That was the nickname for the boss. I hadn't seen that side of him; plus, he'd given me a job, so... But hey, free groceries were free groceries.

"Understood," I chuckled.

I was done for the day, so I left and took the bus toward Olympia Square. I was definitely excited to come home. I had good news and free food. There was also some extra dough I'd pocketed by walking to work a few times, all of which I saved for Willow.

From my understanding, she ran her own business from home. She was happy to watch Thea whenever, but I wasn't stupid. Babysitting didn't pay that well, and I was calling her a lot more often than my aunt ever did. Willow deserved whatever extra cash I could spare.

I stepped off the bus and crossed the square. Adrian should be home already, so maybe I'd missed Willow. In that case, I'd see her on Thursday instead.

The apartment smelled like food, causing my stomach to twist in hunger.

Kicking off my sneakers, I grinned when Thea came running toward me. She crashed into me and hugged my thigh.

"Hey, baby." I picked her up and planted smooches all over her face. It made her giggle. "Did you have a good day?"

She nodded and signed her personal name for Willow followed by, "ice cream" and "playground." Those were the two words I caught, anyway.

"You went to the playground and had ice cream?" I double-checked.

I studied ASL an hour or two a day depending on how much time I had, so it was a slow process. It was also difficult finding a balance between making her comfortable and encouraging her to make sounds.

This time, I got it right. Thea nodded and then she wanted down again.

She skipped after me as I went to the kitchen where I found Adrian.

"Hey." I put the groceries on the counter. "Marla gave me this. Cool, huh?"

He eyed the groceries I unpacked. "That's great. How was work?"

"It was good." It was my turn to eye him. "Are you okay? Wait, don't answer that." I distracted myself by stowing away the groceries and doing my best to follow what Thea was signing to me.

Truth was, I worried. Adrian seemed more tired these days, and it had to be about me. I wasn't doing enough.

His lack of enthusiasm had prompted me to ask if he was okay too often. He always said he was, and I always doubted him.

If I could just find another job, I'd be able to pitch in more. I turned Adrian down every time he offered to watch Thea, I'd started cooking for myself and Thea when he wasn't home, I did my best to clean and keep shit tidy, and I retreated to my room with my girl whenever Adrian sat down to work at the dining room table.

So it had to be about money. Maybe he'd been dipping into savings to help me, and he was running out.

"Dinner's ready." He filled two plates with meatloaf, mashed potatoes, gravy, and steamed vegetables. For Thea, who didn't eat meatloaf and couldn't stand the texture of gravy, he'd made a fancy version of mac and cheese.

The guilt crushed heavier and harder.

"I could've made her dinner," I said.

He paused, brow furrowed, his mouth set in a firm line. "Do you mind that I do it?"

"No, of course not—"

"Neither do I." He took his plate and went to the living room.

He was okay, fucking *sure*.

Throughout dinner, he was correcting papers while Thea and I discussed her starting in a playgroup. I glanced over at Adrian every now and then, wanting to include him, but I wouldn't interrupt when he was busy.

Thea tapped my arm and slid me a note.

"Willow said the children can't hear," it said.

"That's right." I nodded. "It's a small playgroup. Most are deaf." If I saved and kept working my ass off, I'd be able to afford it after the summer. "You'd make friends who are starting to learn sign language. That's good, huh?"

She was overdeveloped in that particular area, though she'd still get more out of playing with those kids than the ones she tried to befriend at the playground. Plus, the teacher or whatever had the right education for all that shit.

Thea signed something I didn't understand; she formed a

strange version of the letter "C" and tapped it to her shoulder. I asked her to explain.

At that, Adrian spoke. "It's her sign name for me."

My brows rose. "She made you a name?"

He nodded, never looking up from the test he was taking the infamous red pen to.

"What does it mean?" My eyes flicked between him and Thea.

Thea beamed brighter than the sun, deserted her food, and rounded the table to join Adrian at his side. She formed the "C" again, and he smiled softly at her and did the same sign, bringing them close. But it wasn't a fucking "C" at all. Between their thumbs and forefingers, they each formed half a heart.

"She taps her shoulder," Adrian explained, "because she likes to fill in the tattoo I have there with her markers."

I swallowed, confused and moved. She did what? How come I'd never seen that?

"What about you?" I asked him.

He shifted in his seat, uncomfortable, and got back to work. "I hold it to my chest."

He might as well have said heart.

This kinda fucked me up, and I could barely focus when Thea went back to the topic of the playgroup. She asked if Adrian—using that name for him, obviously—could pick her up from playgroup sometime.

"We'll see," I murmured, distracted.

Staring down at my food, I went sort of blank for a while. I had questions but no answers whatsoever. Adrian and Thea barely spent time together alone, so I had no clue how they'd grown close. Maybe the mornings on the weekends? I did find them in the living room together sometimes. And, of course, the days I worked longer and Willow left before I came home.

Adrian hadn't been comfortable revealing his sign name for

Thea, so I didn't know if that was because he didn't like it or if... I just didn't know. I could only hope he wasn't merely humoring her. 'Cause it was obvious she'd grown attached, though I'd missed it. Fucking idiot that I was. Blind idiot.

After dinner, Thea crawled up in my lap to watch cartoons, and Adrian said he was gonna prepare some food to bring to the Quad. It was all the reminder I needed, and I told Thea I'd be right back. Then I headed after Adrian to the kitchen.

"I'll go with you on Thursday," I said, filling the sink with hot water so I could do the dishes.

He frowned as he brought out ingredients to make bread. "You work then."

"No, I talked to Mike today. He said it's okay if I come down on Friday mornings instead." I stacked a clean plate in the dish rack. "Diego's already let me switch to Fridays, so it'll work out. I do the bar in the morning, and then I think I have like two hours before my shift at Diego's starts."

Adrian hummed, troubled by something. "We appreciate all the help we can get, of course, but then you'd be working every day except for Sundays."

"Like the man upstairs intended it..." I joked. I shrugged and rinsed suds from a glass. "Not really, though. My shifts aren't very long."

Friday would be my busiest day. I would be in Cedar Valley all day, practically. The rest...? The shifts were only a few hours long. That was why I needed another job or two.

"Speaking of Sunday, you haven't forgotten dinner, right?" Adrian asked.

"No, 'course not." I wasn't looking forward to it. His younger brother, AKA Bomber Jacket, was coming over with his girlfriend.

It put me on edge. He'd judge me for sure, and I hadn't

come far enough in life to be comfortable around strangers knowing my business.

The original plan had been for us four to go to a restaurant, and I'd been the pest bitching and moaning about money. I had so little, and I didn't want Adrian to pay for me, which he'd been quick to offer. Then I'd gotten lucky. Willow had plans, so she couldn't watch Thea.

In the end, Adrian had suggested we have dinner here.

"I can't wait to have your family thinking I'm bad for you," I told him with a smirk.

"Wow," he muttered. "You think that highly of them, huh?"

I clamped my mouth shut. *Dominic does it again.* Perhaps being permanently gagged would benefit me.

"That's not what I meant," I said quietly. "I'm sorry." I turned off the water and reached for the towel. "I just know I ain't much to brag about."

It put a rock in the pit of my stomach.

"I beg to differ." Adrian started cracking eggs into a bowl. "You work hard, you provide for your daughter, and you're a good man."

But I didn't provide for Thea. I earned enough now to pay half the food and utilities, not to mention her time with Willow, but rent? There wasn't much I could contribute there.

If it weren't for Adrian, I'd still be on the streets. Thea would be with my aunt and unable to relax.

I hadn't even known what a cheerful and carefree little girl she was until we left Aunt Chrissy's. It was no wonder Thea never asked for her. She was finally happy.

"You're doing well, Dominic. Give yourself a break."

I snorted and dried the last glass. "I will when I can afford it."

I couldn't sleep.

I knew why, too. It'd been days since I snuck into Teach's room, and I fucking missed him. If he said things were okay one more time, I'd beat his ass. Something *was* wrong; I just didn't know what.

Slipping outta bed without waking Thea, I silently made my way out of the room and then paused outside Adrian's.

It was the middle of the night, so he was most likely asleep. I needed the comfort, though, and he'd never complained before. Then again, he never initiated anything, either. It was confusing.

Shit, was he over it, maybe? I guessed I'd sorta assumed... After our first night, we'd kissed a lot—though not enough—and I'd fucked him a few more times. We'd also gotten each other off once or twice in the shower, and he was always game. But if he never took the first step, was that a sign? Should I quit seeking him out for that?

He was like a drug, so it'd be difficult to stop. I was experiencing new things thanks to him, and I found myself wanting to try more. Lately, I'd fantasized about sucking him off. It wouldn't be dirty with him.

Knowing I'd never reach a conclusion on my own, I opened the door to his room and closed it behind me. It was dark, but I knew my way around his bed now.

He stirred but didn't wake up as I joined him under the covers.

"Teach." I slipped a hand down his chest and kissed his shoulder. He always slept on either his side or his stomach, whereas I preferred to sleep on my back. The best part was he slept naked. "Wake up..."

"Hmmmm."

"I gotta ask you somethin'." Pushing down the covers, I got

him in all his sexy glory. I kissed his chest as I wrapped my fingers around his cock and began stroking him slowly.

"What the...fuck?" he grumbled drowsily. "Dominic?"

"Yeah." I licked the V that led to his crotch. There was something about licking and kissing that did it for me. "I have a question."

In the faint moonlight, I could only see the outline of his cock. He groaned under his breath as I stared at it. *I can fucking do this.* Hell, my body wanted it. I could do this right. It was intimate with him. Sex was about pleasure now, not a way to pay for my food.

He woke up fully, startled when I licked the underside of his cock. And once I'd started, I was done for. His hissed curse turned me on, and I closed my mouth around the head of him.

"You don't have to do that," he said quickly, sitting up.

I smirked internally, and then I swallowed him whole.

"Christ!" He fell back again and threw an arm over his face.

It was exciting because I gave a fuck. I *wanted* him to lose his shit when I pleasured him. More than that, it turned me on to suck him off.

"Dominic..." He groaned and wove his fingers into my hair.

"Can I ask my question now?"

"*Now?*" he asked incredulously. "God—fuck, I suppose."

I hummed around his shaft, soaking him in spit and hollowing out my cheeks. "Do you mind that I kiss you? That I come in here some nights?" I sucked on the skin where his thigh met his crotch. He was sensitive there.

He sighed and guided me back to his dick. "No. I can't." He shuddered and moaned and got a filthy fucking mouth. "God*damn*, you can suck cock." Pushing himself up on one elbow, he stared at me hungrily and was in charge of the pace. "That's fucking perfect, baby... Perfect, perfect. Is this making you hard?"

I swallowed around him, squeezing the head, and he sucked in a sharp breath. Then I nodded and shifted so he could feel my dick against his leg. Sucking him faster, I fisted the base of him and grazed my teeth along the thick vein on the underside.

"Fuck." He brushed his thumb over my hollowed out cheek, then down to my bottom lip. "Next time we kiss, I want to taste us."

I closed my eyes and moaned. He put images in my head that made me fucking leak.

"Almost there," he grunted.

While he let go of my head, I redoubled my efforts. I wasn't half-assing this. I'd get every goddamn drop.

Moments later, he exploded with a long groan. Rope after rope of come hit the roof of my mouth until I slid him down my throat again. I swallowed repeatedly, less bothered by the taste than I thought I would be.

Adrian collapsed, panting, and I sucked him clean before I kissed my way up his torso. His warm hands traveled up and down my back, and he was fast to capture my mouth in a breathless kiss.

I was going nuts. We were all tongues and hands and teeth. I couldn't fucking describe what it did to me. I tensed up, only to melt into him. Back and forth, back and forth. Shivers ripped down my spine. I pushed my cock against his thigh, after which he got a firm grip of my ass.

"I could kiss you forever." I swept my tongue across his bottom lip, then sucked it into my mouth. He tasted so good. It was sex, mint, and Adrian.

He let out a low growl as I stroked his jaw. "My turn. Stand up."

He gave my ass a slap, and I couldn't help but laugh. I was losing my marbles around this man. He made me happy, and the rock in my gut was gone when we were together like this.

I left the bed, curious to see what he had planned. It'd been...oh, five or so years since the last time I received head.

Adrian sat up and planted his feet on the floor. "Mouth-watering."

I grinned and had to make a dig. "Well, you know I'm clean."

He rolled his eyes but shook his head in amusement. "Be good."

He had an air of authority in his tone, that teacher voice, and it was hot as fuck in the bedroom.

"You want to." I grabbed my cock and stroked it slowly. "Suck it."

He narrowed his eyes. "Say please, or you'll fucking regret it."

Holy shit.

I swallowed. "Aight... Please. Please suck me."

"Much better," he murmured. Sliding his hands up the back-sides of my thighs, he leaned close and nuzzled the root of my dick. "You smell amazing."

The anticipation was killing me.

"Please," I said again.

He grinned against my skin and gave it a slow kiss. Then he finally wrapped his long fingers around me, and he licked the tip. I bit my lip, tense and shaky.

"Oh my God..." I whispered as he, inch by inch, took me deep. My head fell back, and I closed my eyes. His mouth was heaven—warm and wet, with perfect pressure.

His tongue swirled around me, tracing every ridge. When he took me to the back of his throat, his beard scratched my balls, too. Christ, it was like everything he did made me wanna come. Everything excited me.

My eyes had adapted to the darkness, and when the initial burst of pleasure had settled in me, I eye-fucked Adrian while he went to town on my cock. He sucked me firmly, always coming off so damn sensual and seductive. He didn't rush.

"Shit." I gasped and gripped his shoulders when he palmed my ass and yanked me forward. He moaned around me, which sent vibrations up my cock. "Ohhhfuckme." Unable to help it, I pulled out then pushed back in, and he seemed to like that. "You want me to fuck your mouth?"

He hummed, and it was enough to bring me close. I didn't have the same stamina he did, that was for damn sure.

"I-I won't last long." I fucked him in shallow thrusts, quick ones that sped up my heart rate. "Oh God, Adrian." I swallowed dryly. Every time I slid along his tongue, I thought I was gonna lose it. "I'm—"

I trembled and tensed up. He could tell I was there. The look in his eyes did me in. All wild and commanding. A whimper slipped past my lips, and I surrendered on a breathless moan.

He took all of me and sucked me harder throughout my orgasm. Sweat beaded on my forehead, and I couldn't control my breathing. Hell, I couldn't control anything.

The second I was done, my knees gave out, but he was a step ahead of me. He pulled me down so I straddled him, and he kissed me forcefully, out of breath and possessed.

"So incredibly fucking sexy." He angled his head and kissed me deeper.

I hauled in some much-needed air and tried to catch up. I couldn't, which made for some interesting kissing. It was hot and funny and salty and perfect. I grinned, and he chuckled.

Pushing him back, I followed and got us back under the covers. I needed some of his warmth now.

He sighed and held me close, the way I loved it. "What the hell are you doing to me?"

"I don't know." I scooted even closer and buried my face in the crook of his neck.

I hadn't realized before how safe I felt with him. It was more than merely being comfortable and not feeling threatened. It was rare that he startled me these days. Maybe here and there if he walked up behind me. That was it.

I yawned, my mind at ease. "We should spend more nights together."

"We should, huh?"

I nodded sleepily as my eyes fluttered closed. "You said you didn't mind, and I like this."

It took him a while before he answered. Sleep had almost pulled me under when I heard his quiet voice.

"I like it, too."

11

I was up before the sun the next morning, and it gave me the chance to make breakfast for once. Thea was fussy as fuck, so I didn't have much time for chitchat, and then Adrian had to rush off to work.

He'd been quiet again, pensive, though I hoped last night had bridged whatever gap we'd had between us lately.

I spent the day with my girl. We studied together, went to the playground, and had an epic rap battle. So far, it was the only thing that made her do sounds of her own accord, and it was fun to see her develop an interest in music. If she found comfort in that, it should help her.

Then after Willow showed up, it was my turn to get to work. I took the bus to Cedar Valley and spent the evening cleaning tables and bringing dishes to the kitchen. I got a free dinner and tips, which never failed to make my day.

By the time my shift was over, my feet hated me. Luckily I had an hour's break before I went over to Mike's.

I sat down on a bench outside with chips and salsa from the restaurant and killed some time on my phone. It'd been a while since I heard from Billy; he hadn't responded to my last text, so I fired off another.

Hope everything is good, old man. I still don't believe in Irish luck, but life is turning around. Washington is nice. You should visit.

I attached a selfie I'd taken of Thea and me and pressed send.

While I was at it, I sent one text to Adrian, too.

I thought spring was coming? Brace yourself for my cold feet later.

I grinned and scratched my nose, and then I chuckled at his response.

You're wearing your jacket, right? Your feet are always cold. I'm getting used to it.

Worrywart. I dug it. And of course I was wearing my jacket. Adrian had wanted to buy me one; I'd obviously said no, but I'd graciously accepted one of his old ones. It was a little big, but who cared?

You're always warm. I love it. I've gotten used to it. ;)

Hey, look at me, flirting. Though, "addicted" was more apt than "used."

Adrian didn't answer. It was getting late. He'd probably crashed early.

When I came home around three in the morning, I aimed straight for the shower. It didn't warm me up enough, but it washed away the smell of sweat and beer, and Adrian could take care of the rest.

He grunted and winced when I snuck under the covers, my

head landing on his chest. "Christ, Dominic. Give a man a warning."

"I missed you today," I sighed.

At that, he tightened his arms around me and kissed the top of my head.

It didn't take long for me to fall asleep, and then I was alone in bed when I woke up the next morning by someone yanking on my toe.

It was Thea.

I'd slept too long, I guessed.

"Morning, baby," I said groggily. "Come cuddle."

She shook her head and signed that she was hungry.

I had to admit I was pretty pumped to show up at the Quad. Adrian had gone straight from work, so we were meeting up there. And he wouldn't be the only one showing up with shit for the kids.

Willow, Thea, and I had fucking *baked* today. She'd been in the neighborhood and had shown up two hours early, and we'd hung out a bit more as friends, rather than her just being my girl's sitter. It was fun, and she was as good with baking as Adrian was with cooking.

The minute I'd confessed to wanting to help out more and contribute, she'd suggested making brownies.

I had approximately forty of them in a bag now.

I'd had four already...

As per Adrian's directions, the Camas Quad was located across Kings Park, not too far away from the high school. It was a low brick building, and there were a handful of teenagers standing outside smoking.

No doubt, I'd fit in with them more than the men and women who volunteered.

"Yo, you're new." A guy jerked his chin at me.

"Yo, no shit," I replied flatly.

Opening the door, I stepped inside and looked around. It had a warehouse feel, completely open and a lot of concrete and brick. The kids who came here had obviously helped with various projects, like painting some sections of the walls, creating a café area, and bringing color to picnic tables and lawn chairs.

Everything was divided into smaller areas. Furniture was mismatched and no doubt donated or found.

It was a popular place, I could tell. Billy would've liked it.

Half a dozen boys were shooting pool in one corner, a few were chatting in the café area, but most were gathered farther down where I could see a screen on the wall and a bunch of beanbags on the floor. They were taking turns playing video games.

An older woman walked over to me. "Can I help you?"

"Yeah..." I pulled off my beanie, wondering where Teach was. "I'm looking for Adrian? I'm supposed to help out around hea'."

"Oh, you must be Dominic." She smiled and extended her hand. "I'm Maggie. He said you were coming." I shook her hand, and she gestured toward the back. There was a hallway. "One of the girls asked Adrian to sit in on her first counseling session. They should be done soon. Come on, let me introduce you to the kids."

I trailed after her, not seeing any other adults nearby. It was chill, and the kids were just hanging out, but after seeing Adrian come home with that bruise forming on his body, I knew shit happened, too. Two adults and one counselor weren't enough for the some fifteen teens.

This place would've been robbed had it been in South Philly.

"Girls," Maggie said as we paused by the café. "This is Mr. Cleary. He'll be with us on Thursdays from now on."

It was completely fucked for me being a *mister*. "Uh, Dominic's fine." I gave a two-finger wave.

A couple broads got giggly, and one winked slyly and said, "He sure is."

I smirked faintly. She was what, fifteen? I remembered that age. Add in their reasoning for being at the Quad, and I knew very well I'd get to meet some cocky exteriors. The community centers and soup kitchens I'd been to in New York were a hella lot different, but I did remember all the fronting. I'd walked around with a permanent chip on my shoulder to show I had balls and wasn't afraid.

Maggie rolled her eyes, amused by the girl, and told me I'd get to know them better later. Then we continued to the gaming area, and this time, she introduced me as Dominic.

There was a collective chin nod and a "'sup" from the guys.

Funny thing was, I should've come here sooner 'cause I fucking knew I'd do this well. I knew these kids because I used to be them, all of them, in one way or another.

"Oh, and this—" I extended the plastic bag to Maggie. "Adrian's always bringing shit down here, so I figured I'd do the same."

She peered inside the bag and lifted the lid off one of the containers. "Well, damn. I'm not sure I wanna share. This is lovely. Thank you, Dominic."

One boy perked up. "What you got there, Mrs. H?"

"Wouldn't you like to know?" she teased.

I snorted a chuckle, but it was cut off by a loud snapping sound that bounced off the walls. I whipped around and saw a kid had cracked a pool cue in half and was about to get his ass beat by a dude twice his size.

It was a no-brainer. Maggie was two shits high, and Adrian wasn't around. I had no doubt Maggie could inflict some pain, and people who worked in these joints had to be mentally strong, but even so. It'd be easier for me to break it up.

"Who're you calling maid's boy, huh?" the scrawny kid growled.

I was on my way over before I knew it, and Maggie wasn't far behind.

The bigger boy laughed. "You dumb, too? No wonder your mom's gotta clean rich ass up in Ponderosa. She can't count on you for shit."

"Ay!" I jogged the last distance and stepped in between them right before Scrawny could take a swing. "Back off." I planted a hand on his chest and pushed. "What's the goddamn problem?"

Scrawny glared at the other one. "Ask that fucktard. Cole's always coming here to be a dick."

Cole smirked cockily. "I'm just telling it like it is. Ain't my problem you can't handle the truth."

"And what's that, huh?" I nodded at him.

He shrugged. "You know... His mom's on her knees scrubbing floors like some cheap—"

"Yo, I fucking dare you to finish that sentence." I faced him fully, getting in his personal space and ignoring a murderous Scrawny behind me. "So his mother does what she can to put food on the table, and you piss all over that? What, you here because you're loaded?"

He scowled at me, but I was no kid, and his balls weren't so big anymore. "She could have some pride and not be a Ponderosa bitch."

My brows rose, and I had to laugh. "Oh, check this one out."

I jerked my thumb at him and glanced at the others who were gathering around to watch. "He thinks cleaning is beneath him." Turning to Cole again, I stepped closer and got real serious. "Not everyone can afford pride, but let's make one thing crystal clear, kid. There's no shame in *cleaning rich ass*. We do what we can—" I jabbed a finger at his temple "—so quit bustin' chops and get that through your skull."

Cole gritted his teeth but kept his trap shut. Then he turned around and left when some of the others hooted and hollered and motioned for a mic drop. A bit over the top, maybe. It was cute when my three-year-old daughter did it.

"Welcome to the Quad, Dominic," Maggie said with a wry smile. "Something tells me you'll fit right in." She slid her gaze to Scrawny. "*You*, Gabe, have to stop breaking things here."

As the kids scattered to get back to their video game and whatever, I saw Adrian standing in the back, leaning casually against a wall. He smiled and nodded once at me, and then he went back to the counseling.

I exhaled, relieved, and rubbed a hand over my jaw and mouth to hide my grin.

A while later, I shared a picnic table with four chatty girls who wanted to know everything about growing up in New York. Apparently my accent had given me away...? Their mouths wouldn't stop running. It was cute.

"Have you ever been to Manhattan?" one asked excitedly.

"Sure." I leaned back in my seat and pulled up one foot to rest it on my knee. "Overrated if you ask me, but you get used to the smell."

There was a hand on my shoulder, and I looked up to see Adrian was done with whatever he'd been doing down the hall.

"Hi, Mr. D, have you met Dominic?" a girl named Anna asked. "He's from New York."

"We may have met once or twice." Adrian winked at her and sat down. "Or it's possible he's my roommate."

"Lucky," another broad sighed.

I smirked faintly, side-eyeing my *roommate*. We were more than that, weren't we? I didn't know what, but roommate wasn't enough.

"I'd say Dominic's the lucky one." A girl batted her lashes at Adrian. "Why are all the hot ones gay?"

I barked out a laugh.

"Don't you have homework to do, Sandra?" Adrian asked, amused. "I know for a fact that your teacher is a badass who won't accept another F from you."

Oh. So he was her teacher. Funny.

"Badass Buzzkill," she corrected, moping. Then she sighed dramatically and grabbed her bag to go sit somewhere else. "Who cares what happened in Greece, like, two thousand years ago, *anyway?*"

"Everyone who's a fan of democracy?" I drawled.

"*Thank* you." Adrian clapped me on the back, his hand lingering while he spoke to Sandra. "And let's not forget the greatest philosophers—"

"Oh, here we go!" a few of them exclaimed.

That shit cracked me up. "See, this is why I call you Teach."

"Well, I *am* a teacher, and damn proud of it." He scoffed, pretending to be mad 'cause his lecture was cut short. I wanted to fucking kiss him. He was...I didn't even know, but I couldn't tear my eyes away. "Now, go make yourselves useful, ladies. You all have homework. If you keep it down and do well, I hear there are brownies for later." He squeezed my leg under the table, the corners of his mouth twisting up.

The girls scampered off with their textbooks and backpacks, leaving me alone with Adrian.

"Hey." I grinned and rested my forearms on the table, and he mirrored my movement. "I like watching you with these kids."

"Yeah?" He chuckled, looking down at the table, and loosened his tie. "I enjoy being here."

I could tell.

"I think I'm gonna like it here, too." I looked out over the open space, teenagers scattered all over. If I could help any of them, even if it was just one, it'd be worth it.

Adrian may have been the reason I came, but I had a feeling that would change once I learned more about the backgrounds of some of these children.

I should've realized it sooner that they'd be much like me.

"You handled Cole perfectly," he murmured. "They'll respect you in no time." Mirth flashed in his eyes. "It took me at least two months before they decided I could handle them."

I snorted, 'cause that shit was funny. I had a big mouth and intimidated more people by being cocky, though I sure as hell could hold my own and then some. But Adrian was peaceful. Getting into a fight was an absolute last resort, and if he did, he'd drop the fucker swiftly.

"Can I kiss you here, or do we gotta keep it professional?" I asked quietly.

His eyes showed bewilderment. "Would you even want to?"

I frowned. "Why the fuck wouldn't I?"

He sighed and ran a hand through his hair. For a minute, he looked older than he was. "I don't know, Dominic," he replied tiredly. "I don't know much of anything that goes through your head. I consider asking you every day, but I'm not sure I want the answers."

I didn't know what to say to that, and it was confusing that...

whatever it was...made him look troubled. In other words, I didn't know what the issue was.

"Answers about what?" I wondered. "I'm an open book where you're concerned, Teach. You know the worst about me, so..." I lifted one shoulder. "I got nothin'a hide."

He pursed his lips and then blew out a breath and gave my arm a squeeze. "I'm not making any sense. I suppose I'm worried about the future, but I'm not willing to risk the present by discussing it. Which means I'm fucked, essentially." He smiled ruefully and stood up. "I'm going to make rounds. Do you mind checking in with the boys outside?"

"No, sure." I was still confused about...all that, what he'd said, but I wouldn't push if he didn't wanna talk. "Be good during your rounds and you might get a brownie later."

He laughed, and then he leaned close and his eyes took on a dark glint. "I already have plans to eat one off of you when we get home."

I swallowed.

12

Sunday rolled around, and twenty minutes before Bomber Jacket and his girlfriend were due to arrive, I was nervous as fuck. So much so, I almost missed the fact the dining room table had been cleared of Adrian's work shit.

I'd cleaned the entire apartment aside from that part, and he'd taken care of it while I'd showered. Running a towel over my head, I checked the oven while Adrian was teaching Thea to set the table. They were adorable as hell together, but the worry of her being too much for him always lurked in the background.

"Baby, you wanna help me do the garlic bread?" I asked.

She shook her head, carefully placing the forks and knives by the plates.

Adrian frowned to himself and followed Thea with napkins and wineglasses.

He looked fucking amazing. The jeans fit just right, and the sleeves of his black button-down were rolled up past his elbows. One of his tattoos had been filled in with purple and green markers—a Thea Cleary original—which kinda made him ten times hotter. If he'd stop frowning, I could maybe enjoy the moment more.

"Lemme know if you want me to take her, aight?"

He shook his head and sighed. "How many times do I have to tell you, Dominic?" Always once more, I guessed. "I love spending time with her."

"Okay." I wasn't convinced, but I let it go.

The chicken was nearly done, so I hurried with the bread and cut it into thin slices. Then I retrieved the garlic butter I'd prepared from the fridge and spread it generously on each slice. After that, I dumped a shit-ton of mozzarella, cream cheese, chives, more garlic, and more cheese into a bowl. I mixed it together, and by the time Adrian walked over to take the chicken outta the oven, the cheese was ready to go in.

I checked the recipe about a dozen times to make sure I'd done it right.

The buzzer in the hallway went off, causing me to stiffen up.

"I'll go get dressed," I muttered.

They were here.

Once in my room, I threw the towels in the hamper and stepped into my jeans. Then I put on the first item of clothing I'd bought in ages. A fitted, long-sleeved tee. Black, simple. I could wear it for dinner and at work.

A murmur of voices traveled down the hall as I stumbled into my socks. It was duty calling. I would've stalled if I didn't have an anxious three-year-old to be there for.

Adrian had told her all kinds of shit about Justin and...I wanted to say, Lola...? Either way, Thea had expressed she was excited about our dinner, though I also knew that could change quickly.

Running a hand through my hair, I exited my room and joined everyone who'd gathered in the kitchen. And I'd been right about Thea. She wasn't comfortable whatsoever, but I should've known Adrian had it covered.

He was carrying her. She had her head buried against his neck, her arms trying to reach around him. Adrian was...multi-tasking, basically. Chatting casually with Justin and Lola, all while rubbing soothing circles along Thea's back.

"Speaking of," Adrian said as he spotted me. He smiled and nodded at a pretty girl my age with purple hair. "I was telling Lola that you claimed the staff at Diego's restaurant could be better. She's looking for a job."

I found my balls and walked closer. "They're shitty as fuck," I replied bluntly and extended my hand. "Good to meet'chu, I'm Dominic."

She grinned. "Lola. Nice to meet you, too. We've heard a lot about you." She winked at Adrian, who rolled his eyes.

I glanced over at Justin. He hadn't changed. He was rocka-billy personified.

"You've met my youngest brother already." Adrian shifted Thea to his other hip and checked the rice.

I jerked my chin at Justin, and I was a bit surprised when he reached out to shake my hand, too. I'd gotten the feeling he didn't care for me much. Although, he could just be doing it to be polite now.

"Long time, no see." He smirked faintly. "Your girl's adorable."

Thea. Safe topic. I could do that.

I exhaled and mustered a polite smile. "No argument from me."

It hit me that I didn't know exactly what Adrian had told his family about me. Only that I was the homeless motherfucker they'd given a ride from Seattle.

"Is there anything we can do?" Lola offered.

"You can sit down and relax," Adrian told her pointedly. "Dominic and I got this."

"Hey, you don't have to twist my arm," Justin said. He

ushered his girlfriend to the table, and they took their seats while I got my ass in gear.

Despite how much I wanted to offer to take Thea from Adrian, I didn't. I kept my mouth shut and put the bread in the toaster, took out the mozzarella dip, and assisted him with whatever he needed.

The chicken was soaked in spicy sauce and vegetables, and the smell made my stomach snarl.

"Fuck, this looks good." Automatically, I leaned over and kissed his jaw.

His mouth twitched, and he shook his head to himself. "You just outed yourself, so you know."

Oh. Well, what the fuck did I care? I had nothing to hide.

My only concern was him. I didn't know if I'd offended him or some shit.

"Are we a secret?" I asked quietly.

That would sting, but I'd get it. I was no grand prize.

"I don't even know what *we* are." There was a hint of frustration in his tone, though before I could process his question and answer, he carried the chicken over to the table.

I made a mental note to ask him later, and then I followed him with the rice and the dip.

"You want to sit with me or with Daddy?" he murmured to Thea.

I got the last of the food, and she decided Adrian was the best today. We never sat at the table, so I hadn't even considered getting her a high chair, but I had a feeling she wasn't complaining.

"This looks *amazing*." Lola beamed and fanned out her napkin over her lap. "I'm glad we didn't go to a restaurant. Holy crap, Adrian."

"I hope it tastes as good as it looks." Adrian smiled, more

focused on Thea. He appeared happy she'd wanted to sit with him, so I relaxed for now.

I didn't talk much through dinner 'cause I was starving. It was interesting to watch Adrian interact with Justin and Lola, though. They were close and knew a lot about each other, and Lola seemed to have been around the Dalton family a while.

There was a brief moment of pride for me when Justin said the garlic bread and mozzarella dip was "fucking spectacular," and I made sure to mention it was Adrian's recipe when he gave me all the credit. I wasn't comfortable with that. Lord fucking knew, had I been in charge of cooking tonight, we'd be eating mac and cheese.

Thea became fussy when she tried the food. It took a minute, but we eventually understood the texture of the sauce wasn't good for her. She went nuts for dipping the chicken in the cheese instead, so it was a win, anyway.

"I'm stuffed." Lola slumped back and patted her belly. "That was so good, you guys."

"Bro, do you mind...?" Justin jerked his thumb over his shoulder. "Or I can go downstairs."

"No, use the fire escape." Adrian shrugged. To me, he explained, "He's just going to smoke."

Fuck.

It'd been months... I refused to buy, though. I had more important things to spend money on.

"And when're you going to quit, babe?" Lola sang.

Justin chuckled and stood up. "Monday, as always." He eyed me, lifted a brow, and held out his pack. "You look interested, man."

No shit.

I flicked my gaze to Adrian. He was understandably confused and surprised.

"Fuck this." I threw my napkin on the table and rose from my seat. "I have no willpower. You can give me a lecture later, Teach."

"Oh, I see." Adrian kissed Thea on the forehead. "We're avoiding Daddy later. He's going to be nasty."

Her giggle made my heart soar. I loved that sound. Then I happily followed Justin to the living room and outside to the fire escape.

"Thanks." I accepted a smoke from him. "My first in months."

"Damn." Justin lit his up and then handed me the lighter. "Why cave now?"

I shrugged and took a slow drag. "It's more of an indulgence at this point. I don't buy 'em." It was a regular cigarette, but given how rarely I smoked these days, it tasted strong at first. "Back in New York—shit, you won't get a pack under twelve bucks."

Philly was cheaper, not that it mattered.

I tilted my head up to blow out some smoke.

"So...you and my brother, huh?"

I walked right into that one, didn't I? I made a face and cocked a brow. "What about us?"

He didn't make me nervous. For one, I could take him if it came to that. For two, he'd been nice but not overly so during dinner. My people-reading skills hadn't rusted up yet, so I trusted my gut.

Justin smirked and took a drag. "Don't play him, that's all."

"I wouldn't." I frowned, the nicotine giving me a quick rush. "If anything, I'm waiting for him to think we're too much."

"You and your girl?" He peeked inside, then shook his head. "Not gonna happen. He's sold."

"How can you know that?" My question kinda rushed out of me.

"Because he doesn't do casual." Justin eyed me, as if debating something with himself. "Look, Adrian's one of the smartest people I know. He's also got this bleeding heart that will drain him with the wrong person. You're not the first one he's offered shelter to, and some have taken advantage in the past."

That explained a lot. I'd told Adrian he was stupid for offering for me to stay here without knowing me, and he had admitted he'd made some foolish decisions in the past. Then he'd said he didn't think this was one of them.

"I don't know what makes you and your daughter different," Justin said, "but you definitely are."

"What do you mean?"

He shrugged. "Bleeding heart or not, he's got limits. He won't bend over backward for someone who gives fuck-all in return. But for you and Thea, I don't think there's much he wouldn't do."

That made sense. My own impression of Adrian was that he believed there was good in people, and he was willing to risk his feelings getting hurt to prove it—for a while. Like Justin said, Adrian was smart. He wouldn't be fooled for an extended period of time. But he sure as hell put others before himself and would undoubtedly give second and maybe even third chances.

"I guess if you two are dating, that's all the difference that matters." Justin flicked away some ash.

Dating.

My forehead creased, and I hesitated. I knew *of* dating. Never actually done it, nor did I know the boundaries. What constituted dating? I hadn't taken him to the fucking movies or anything.

"I'm not sure we're dating," I said. "We live together, and we...yeah."

He snorted. "Then give the guy some reassurance." *Reassurance?* He went on, 'cause the question was written all over me. "If he doesn't know where you two are, figure it out and tell him —stat. He's told me you've got a shitty past, maybe not in those words, but you know. He won't push. He won't assume anything. He'll just hope for the best." He paused. "With a kid involved, I bet that's painful."

I winced at the thought of hurting Adrian, and something hit me that made me wanna throw my bum-ass off a cliff. Every time I told him I could take Thea, every time I interrupted them for fear he was gonna think we were too much...oh, fuck. I wasn't sparing him. I was hurting him. I made him feel excluded.

"Shit." I took a final drag and threw away the smoke. "That motherfucker. He should know by now I'm fucking clueless. He's gotta be upfront, or I won't get it."

Justin chuckled.

We returned inside, and my mind was fucked. I'd been society's outcast for so long that I couldn't picture myself having a normal life. My existence had been about survival, not about getting through the weeks and looking forward to weekends where I could chill with buddies and go on dates. Even now, just thinking about it...I wasn't sure. I wasn't sure I'd ever be that guy.

My phone rang as Justin and Lola were getting ready to leave, so I excused myself to see if it was Billy finally returning my call.

It was.

"Where the fuck have you been?" I sat down on the edge of my bed.

He laughed quietly, sounding tired. "Hey to you, too." He paused. "I've been meaning to call, but I've had a lot goin' on."

"Kids giving you grief?" I asked.

Much like at the Quad, fights could happen at Billy's place. Those were more vicious, too. Everyone who lived on the street tried to have means to defend themselves, be it knives or pipes—anything. I'd broken up a fight or thirteen in my days. Been part of several, as well. Had the scars to show for it.

"No." He cleared his throat. "I left Philly last week."

"Wait, what? Why?"

"Because, ah..." He was stalling, and it put me on edge. That wasn't Billy. He cut the shit and got straight to the point. "I got some bad news, kid. Looks like I got cancer."

His words traveled through me slowly, draining the blood from my face and punching nausea into me. My brain was slow to catch up, 'cause I didn't fucking want to.

Cancer.

It'd spread to his liver, he told me.

Something about his lymph nodes...

It was impossible.

"There're treatments," I heard myself mumble.

My hands were clammy and cold. Head buzzing. One trigger away from vomiting all over the floor.

"At this point, it's useless," he answered patiently. "Doctors say I have three to six months. I don't wanna spend that time with my head in the toilet."

I shook my head, unable to process. I could count the number of people I was attached to on one hand. Losing one of them...?

"I'm staying with my brother in Florida now," he went on. "I get to see my nieces, too. It's good for me."

"But you can't fucking die," I blurted out. And with those

words, something inside me cracked wide open. I covered my mouth, and my vision grew blurry.

I was swimming in memories. They were all awful, but Billy was a bright spot in each one. The times I'd stumbled into his place, beat-up and bloody. The times he'd heated up soup in the middle of the night because the Philly winters had turned me—and the other guys—into walking frostbite.

He'd never had much to give, but it'd been enough.

"It's okay, Dominic."

"It's not," I croaked. "Fuck." I squeezed my eyes shut. "This ain't right. You and your Irish fucking luck, you're supposed to..." *not die.*

He chuckled. "Yeah... Maybe you were right about that one. But I have no regrets. I did the best I could with what I got."

I couldn't help it; I snapped at him. "Can you quit talkin' like you got one foot in the goddamn grave already?"

"But I do, kid," he implored. "Don't be stupid now."

"I can't afford to go see you." That upset me, and I crumpled. Months ago, I would've been stoic. Death was part of life, and weakness got you killed faster. I'd become soft. Leaning forward, I cried silently into my hand and hated the world.

Billy was *good*, dammit.

"What good would that do?" he responded. "No, you finally have a life. Do me a favor and live it. Nothing would make me happier."

I tried and failed to speak.

"I'd forbid it, anyway," he grunted. "You don't think I've been mushy about this call already? I've dreaded it. You were always special to me." He cleared his throat and sniffled. "Fucking hell. No, this is best."

Maybe he was right. Adrian would lend me the money, no doubt. Seeing Billy, though? I'd fucking break.

"Tell me about'chu, Dominic. I wanna know what you're up to. How's Thea?"

"Gimme a minute." I stifled a whimper and tried to breathe right. It took a while. I had the word "cancer" running on a loop in my head, and I wanted to sob like a goddamn baby.

It wasn't fair.

Eventually, I managed to pull my shit together, and I told him this and that about Adrian, work, and Thea's progress. I had to take breaks whenever I thought about never sharing stuff like this with Billy again.

He was a reserved, rough around the edges, stubborn man with a huge heart. Thea would've liked him.

"You and this Adrian...you guys serious?" Billy asked.

I wiped my cheek with the back of my hand. "I don't know what that means."

He laughed gruffly. "Lemme dumb it down for ya, kid. Did'ju find love?"

"Oh..." I sniffled, the word foreign to me. I loved Thea, of course. Whatever I felt for Adrian was different, which I assumed it was supposed to be. "I don't know? I don't know what the fuck I'm doing. We had dinner with his brother tonight, and he asked me a bunch'a shit I couldn't answer, either. It's not like I can be a regular goddamn boyfriend."

His amusement faded, and the next time he spoke, his tone was gentler. "Who says you have to? From what you've told me about Adrian, he seems understanding and down-to-earth. If he's into you, maybe he's not looking for regular."

I chewed on my lip. What did I have to offer but myself? Could that really be enough? He could get anyone.

"Are you getting sappy on me, Billy?"

"Ha!" His laugh made him cough dryly. "Well, maybe. There's you and a couple other boys who've made an impact on me the most over the last five or six years. Knowing you're happy would mean a lot to me."

My bottom lip trembled, tears welling up all over again. "Shit." I couldn't handle this. Stab me, rob me, tear up my fucking ass, but don't take Billy.

"So, do you love this fucker or not, kid?" he pressed.

I blew out a heavy breath. "Maybe? Fuck if I know. It's kinda hard to think about that when you're fucking dying." I broke at that and began weeping.

"Dominic," he said thickly.

I shook my head even if he couldn't see it and rubbed my eyes. "I don't know what to say. The only time I've ever thought about the future was, you know, to have it as a goal to get off the streets and have a place for me and Thea." I reached for a tissue and wiped my nose. "Now all I can think of is not sharing shit with you. And I know that's selfish, but whatever. You saved my damn life, and Adrian's turning it into a good life to live. He's home, you know? But it's like..." I tried to come up with a decent analogy, and all I got was: "You're the photo album, you fucker. I'm supposed to be able to bring it out whenever I have a new memory to store. You're that guy—" I stopped when it hit me.

He was no photo album. The reason I called him when I had stuff to talk about was because that's what kids did with their parents. A guy went off to college. When he scored high on a test or met someone, he called his folks. Right?

"I know, Dominic," he said quietly. "I know."

He probably did. I was the one who was always late to understand basic crap.

He sighed. "Now do you get why I wanna make sure you're doing all right?"

I nodded, forgetting he couldn't see me. "Yeah," I mumbled. "I'm doing well, though. I promise. I like working, I have a real home—"

"About that." He hummed. "You said Adrian's your home."

I did?

I did.

Thinking about it, I shrugged. "I guess it's the only thing that makes sense to me. He's safe and comforting, he makes me happy, and I'm...yo," I chuckled, "I'm like a stalker. I'd rather watch him than the TV." I scratched my neck. "I'm weird, I know. He's great with Thea, too. And he might know more sign language than I do right now, but he learns mad fast."

"See, that's the shit I wanna hear!" There was a smile in his voice now. "Go on. I can't sleep, anyway. Tell me more."

I hadn't considered the time difference. It was late on the East Coast, though I wasn't about to deny him. Whether I was laughing or I had tears streaming down my face, I told Billy anything I could remember and think of.

It was cleansing and depressing at once. He was confident I was in love, and maybe it was wishful thinking. Maybe it wasn't. One thing was certain, though. I was gonna put it all out there for Adrian so he knew I wasn't using him or was interested in just sex.

"Anything I can do?"

I shook my head and sniffled for the hundredth time. Adrian was holding me tightly under the covers in his bed, and that was perfect. All I needed.

He'd verbally torn me a new one when I'd apologized for being a pussy. After that, I'd broken down and stopped giving a flying fuck. That said, I was tired of crying and wished I could pull it together already.

It was four in the goddamn morning. Or it was, last time I checked.

Adrian had work...

I didn't start until later.

"I hate seeing you this way," he whispered against my temple. "And I honestly don't see why you won't go see him."

It was unbelievably tempting. I got the feeling Billy was serious about not seeing me, though. I'd brought it up again before we hung up, and he'd been quiet, then mentioned he'd changed. He was losing weight and had grown physically weaker. At the same time, who gave a shit?

I'd never hugged him. I should've hugged him at the Greyhound station.

"If you're hesitating because of money...I swear to Christ, Dominic."

"I'm not," I muttered. It was sorta true. I hated borrowing, but this wasn't the time or place to worry about that. "I'm just a chickenshit. If I see him, I won't be able to hold it together."

"So?" he asked, frustrated. "You're not really holding it together now, either."

I scowled and lifted my head to face him. "Thank you, for pointing *that* out."

His mouth twisted up and he cupped my cheek, his thumb brushing away a tear. "I don't want either of you to regret anything. Something tells me he's as stubborn as you are." He kissed me on the forehead. "At the risk of overstepping, I want you to know I'm more than willing to go with you. Easter is just around the corner, so I'll have some time off."

"Fuck," I breathed out. "*Yes*." It clicked. Sealed the deal. I couldn't turn that shit down. "You're not playin'? You'd seriously go with me? Us—Thea, too."

He laughed, his voice both whiskey and silk, and shook his head. "You truly have no idea, do you?" He pressed his forehead to mine. "I want to go with you."

Okay. Good. That was good. A huge relief.

I'd call Billy tomorrow. He'd put up a fight and bitch at me, but it was simple. Either he fesses up and gives me his address, or I hunt him down.

One issue. "How do I get a passport or an ID for the plane?"

"Hmm." He looked pensive. "If I'm not mistaken, we can pay extra to have them delivered faster. We'll take care of it."

I shrugged and lay down again on his chest. "Or we'll take the bus."

"Let's hope it won't come to that."

I chuckled.

Then I sighed, content, and pressed a kiss to his pec. "Thank you."

"For what?"

For being the one I called my pseudo dad to talk about.

For giving me more than I could ever dream of.

For turning a homeless guy into someone who looked forward to waking up in the morning.

For becoming my home.

Take your pick.

"For everything, Teach."

13

The following Thursday, being at the Quad didn't feel as satisfactory anymore. I guessed I couldn't stop thinking about Billy—everything he'd done—and how we weren't doing enough.

While the kids who hadn't eaten today inhaled the soup Adrian had prepared last night and stuffed their faces with sandwiches Maggie had brought, I presented my idea to Adrian, Maggie, and Marcela—the counselor.

It was just the four of us at a picnic table, so I spoke freely. And bluntly.

"I mean, seriously, some of these teenagers aren't only here to kill time because they're bored at home," I said. "They're not all here because their folks are absent." If that were the case, we wouldn't need Marcela here. "Some get beat up and taken advantage of."

Maggie frowned and stirred a spoon in her coffee mug. "We know that. We're doing our best to provide a safe place for them."

I nodded. "But the reality is that a few of these kids will run away from home at some point. What're we doing for them?"

Adrian sat quietly, pensive.

Marcela pointed toward the bulletin board. "We have families from the church who offer a place to stay."

"And that shit comes with intervention from social services, drug tests, and a future relocation to foster families," I said. "Look, I've been there. I didn't actually run away, but I had nowhere to go 'cause my home situation was fucked up." I leaned forward. "I lived on the streets rather than become a pawn in the system. Kids who get let down by their parents like that...? We stop trusting adults."

Adrian rubbed his jaw and glanced out over the Quad, no doubt seeing what I saw. They had enough experience and training to detect abuse just by watching a kid's behavior. I came from a world of those children.

"What're you suggesting?" Teach tilted his head at me.

"We prepare them," I replied. "I'm not saying we should teach them Dumpster diving and how to keep warm at night, but they'd fare better if they knew what they were facing." I paused and drank the last of my coffee. "I was on my own with no knowledge of how the world worked, so you get these kids who're more suited for a part in *Lord of the Flies* than modern society."

"I see your point." Marcela folded her arms over her chest and nodded thoughtfully. "Many do feel isolated already. Mom and Dad become *them*. Soon after that, all grown-ups fall under the same category."

Word.

"So what do we do?" Maggie asked.

"We teach them how to fish," Adrian responded, amused. I grinned 'cause I was on the inside of that joke. The other two weren't, so he explained the analogy he'd used on me once. "Give a man a fish, and he's fed for a day..."

"'Teach him how to fish, and he's fed for life." Marcela smiled. "Suggestions?"

"How to look for work," Maggie said. "Writing a resume."

Marcela jotted that down on a notepad.

"Bridging the gap between adults and children is important." Adrian hummed. "We're a community, so we need to be inclusive. Rather than us bringing food to the Quad, we should be making it together."

I liked that one.

"Self-defense," I added. My suggestions were bound to be a bit more extreme 'cause of what I'd lived through. "A few stickers and pamphlets on saying no to drugs ain't enough, either. They gotta know the reality. Once you're stuck, you're stuck. Your entire day revolves around finding money for your next fix. You get sick, you share needles, you end up dead."

We continued discussing the changes we could make at the Quad, and I felt marginally better. Apparently, certain days here had themes. Fridays were movie nights. The local church was in charge on Sundays. Tuesdays were for fucking crafts...? To each their own. If making papier-mâché ornaments was part of making this a safe place for kids, by all means. But it wasn't enough, and I was glad Thursdays were gonna change a bit from now on.

"Excuse me." I stood up when I saw one of the girls was about to leave. "I'll be right back."

I followed Amber outside, and she smirked up at me.

"How did it go?" I asked.

"I told you. I do the inventory, so he has no clue." She opened her backpack.

Amber had come up to me when I was working at the store the other day, and I'd taken a break at the sight of her split lip, hidden poorly underneath makeup. We'd talked a bit. She didn't come to the Quad 'cause she was shit-poor and didn't eat. Her parents were doing fairly well; her dad was a florist and ran his own shop in Cedar Valley, and her mom was a homemaker.

That dad was also an abusive drunk.

After school, Amber worked in his shop, and she got fuck-all for it. So I'd had an idea.

It wasn't something I'd run by Maggie and Marcela, that's for sure.

"Here you go." She carefully pulled out a flower wrapped in paper from her bag. "One white rose."

"How much do I owe ya?" I accepted the flower and pulled out my wallet.

"A dollar seventy-five plus tax," she said frankly.

I rolled my eyes and slapped a five into her hand. "You're not putting that in the register. It's for you. Don't alert the IRS."

She giggled and pocketed the money. "Thank you so much. Who's the rose for?"

I smiled wryly. "I think he's your history teacher."

She gaped at me. "Whoa. You're asking out Mr. D?"

"Yup. Wish me luck." I fucking needed it. I had help from Willow and Thea, and I hoped Adrian would accept what I could give. I'd thought about this goddamn date for days. This was what I could do.

"You'll be fine," Amber said. "I've seen him check out your butt."

I let out a laugh. "Well, no need for me to worry, then."

When the Quad closed for the night, Adrian and I walked home together. I'd kept the wrapped flower hidden in the sleeve of my jacket, but now I just held it—and maybe did a few tricks—and I wasn't surprised when he inquired about it.

"Are you going to tell me what that is?" he asked.

I concentrated, trying to balance the end of the stem in my palm. It wasn't one of those roses with mad long stems, so I was pretty good, I thought. "Sure, but not yet." The weather was finally improving. Tonight I wasn't freezing my ass off. Maybe Washington had spring, after all. "Damn." The rose tipped over, so I grabbed it before it hit the ground. "So tonight went well, right?"

Billy would approve when we ambushed him next week. Okay, ambushed was a strong word, though he sure as hell hadn't given up his address without a fight.

I was getting antsy and had nightmares about losing him before we got there.

"Definitely." Adrian eyed the rose and loosened the scarf around his neck. "I want to bring this up with Maggie's husband. You could say he runs the Quad, and he's one of the few employed there and working full time."

"Okay...?"

He went on. "If they're hiring soon, I want them to consider you. I think you could have a profound impact on the entire community. The rest of us may have education on our side, but you know more about where the kids are coming from. You relate, whereas we try to understand."

I was flattered, not to mention humbled. "I can't speak for everyone."

"That may be," he agreed, "but you can do more good with these teenagers than you do at Diego's restaurant. What you said today..." He chuckled quietly. "It's exactly what we need, Dominic."

I swallowed and stared at the ground as we crossed Kings Park.

He had no idea how much that meant to me. To think my past could be useful and help others would be an indescribable relief.

"Thank you." My face felt hot, but at the same time, I was ten feet taller.

Shit like this made me hopeful, and I had to grin.

And fuck waiting until we got to our building. I began unwrapping the flower, and Adrian chided me for dropping some paper on the ground.

"Let's give at least two fucks about the environment, shall we?" He picked it up and tossed it into a nearby trash can.

"You're so perfectly you, Teach. You know that?" I fisted his coat and pulled him down for a hard kiss.

He chuckled, surprised and confused. "Thanks? And ditto."

This was it. We were almost at Olympia Square, but I didn't wait. He'd say yes, right?

"So, yeah, here." I revealed the rose from behind my back, and his eyebrows lifted. "Look, I wanna do that date thing with you, but I barely know how." I cleared my throat, nervous. My stomach twisted. "I'd like to try, though. If you're into restaurants and going to the movies, we'll do that. I'll do my best not to worry about money. 'Cause what it comes down to is I wanna make you happy." I waved a finger between us. "Like you do with me, I mean."

Adrian had been difficult to read throughout my rant, but he smiled softly at the last part, and he leaned close, pressing our foreheads together.

"First of all," he murmured, "you just made my day. Hell, make that year." Oh, good. "Second of all, while I'm certainly not opposed to having dinner out once in a while, I don't need dates, Dominic. I need commitment."

"What do you mean?" I needed to know.

He released a breath and ushered me over to one of the concrete tables and benches, and he leaned back and half sat on the cold tabletop. With his legs parted a bit, he drew me close to stand between them.

"Commitment to me means we belong to each other." He touched my cheek. "We trust each other, stay loyal, support one another, and share everything. If you need something, I want to be the one you go to, and vice versa." A crease formed across his forehead. "I enjoy being in relationships very much, but the feelings I've developed for you terrify me." He brushed a finger over the rose petals. "I'm scared shitless I'll wake up one day to find you and Thea gone, and I constantly worry I put too much pressure on you. That's...new to me, feeling something so intensely."

"Okay." I... Shit. I despised whatever had made him worry so much, and it was probably me. "Um, I haven't felt any pressure. And for the record—'cause I've been thinking about this—the only reason I've been reluctant to let you be with Thea is almost the same. I've been waiting for you to think it's too much."

Adrian let out a choked laugh and rolled his eyes. In that brief moment when he looked up, I saw his eyes were glistening a little.

"Couldn't be further from the truth, Dominic."

I realized he was feeling vulnerable, and I didn't like that, either. It made me wanna protect him. "Hey." I leaned in and stole a quick smooch. "I wanna do that—the commitment. It sounds perfect to me."

He kissed me hard, deeply, *possessively*. It owned me. I guessed, in more ways than one, he owned me, too.

"Are you sure? You've only just started living on your own terms—"

I nodded and cut him off by biting his bottom lip.

He hissed and squeezed my ass.

I grinned. "I'm sure, ya big sack'a worry. Gimme an hour or two in bed tonight, and I'll make sure you never have to doubt me again."

His look said it all. *Count me in.* He kissed me again, slower this time. I melted into him and tilted my head as I stroked his tongue with mine.

"Thank you for the flower."

I laughed under my breath. Said flower was mangled in between us, and I couldn't say I cared.

"I wanted to do something silly," I murmured.

He hummed and pecked me a few times. "Perfectly silly and sweet. Where did you get it?"

"Dominic?" someone called behind me.

I frowned and looked over my shoulder. *Figured.* It was a miracle I hadn't run into my aunt before now. Especially since I worked at the only grocery store in the area.

Aunt Chrissy had just stepped off the bus across the square, probably coming from work, and she looked the same.

"Would that be your infamous aunt?" Adrian asked.

I nodded.

He straightened and his hands disappeared from my ass, though I didn't budge an inch. I had nothing to hide.

"'Sup?" I jerked my chin when she was close enough.

She eyed me, then Adrian, then how close we were. "Same old. You?"

"All good." And I fucking meant it, too. "Perfect, even."

She sniffed. "This your sugar daddy? Always suspected you was queer."

I snorted and squeezed Adrian's hand. "As of two minutes ago, I think boyfriend is the proper term, but you can go with whatever you want."

"We'll see how long that'll last," she replied dryly. "But, you know where I live. We can have the same arrangement when you come crawling back."

I rolled my eyes and told her to fuck off while Adrian just looked irritated.

"So that was my aunt," I said when she'd left.

He slid his gaze to mine. "Charming."

"Isn't she?" I smirked and stepped back, his hand still in mine. I could get used to this. "Let's go home. I still have a date planned."

"You do?" He was surprised.

"Yeah. What, you thought the rose was it?" I scrunched my nose.

He shrugged. "It's more than enough for me." He kissed our linked hands. "I'm not a difficult man to please, Dominic. I lead a simple life because I like it this way." He paused. "A vacation in the summer, though. Nonnegotiable." He sent me a wink. "I'll drag you and Thea along if you fight me on that."

"Vacation...?" I laughed and shook my head. "Nuts, man. My life here is a vacation."

He didn't say anything to that. He only pressed a kiss to the side of my head, and we walked the last distance in comfortable silence.

Seriously, though. *Vacation.* I could conjure up vague images of Thea running around on a beach, which kinda made me smile.

I had a *future* now. Adrian had told me he'd worried about the future. Now he knew, and we were a couple. He didn't need to worry anymore—in that regard, anyway. But it was time for me to realize there even *was* a future. Normal people made plans, had dreams that went beyond getting off the streets, and they worked toward goals. Goals like vacationing.

I barely thought past tomorrow. I suspected that was why I hadn't considered this relationship. I lived day to day and didn't really think about how shit progressed. Now, I could see why he'd been concerned. We were already acting like boyfriends, and, I guessed, when others did that, they set boundaries...? Maybe. They figured out—together—where it was going. If it was leading somewhere.

"Are you hungry?" Adrian asked as we took the elevator up. "I think I could eat a horse."

"I have food covered." Pulling out my phone, I fired off a quick text to Willow.

Home now. Thanks for everything. Call me when you guys wake up.

"There." I pocketed the phone again and grinned nervously. "Now it's just us."

His brows knitted together. "Just us?"

I nodded, stepping out of the elevator. "Thea's having a sleepover at Willow's."

"Hmm. Are you hoping to get lucky?"

That had to be the best opening for the cheesiest line ever. "What're you talkin' about, baby? I'm already lucky."

"Oh, Jesus Christ." He laughed and nudged me into the apartment, and I couldn't help but crack up, too.

Comedy hour ended when Adrian dropped his bag on the table in the kitchen and saw the spread Willow had set up in the living room. I was nervous, but I was sure I'd remembered his favorite snacks.

Living with him had taken me on a goddamn culinary journey, and it had given me some awesome memories, too. Obviously, we couldn't recreate the stellar meals he'd made over these past few months, but we'd done well with snacks and appetizers. Mostly Willow, no lie.

"You've been...busy today..." Adrian walked closer to the coffee table, and I went to get some shit from the fridge. "You did all this while I was at work? Hey, some of this is still warm."

"Let's just say Willow's an angel," I called back. Grabbing the beer Teach preferred, I got milk for myself and the platter of cheese and fruit.

I'd dipped into a week of saved tips to buy it all, but oddly, I didn't feel very guilty. There was a sting, maybe, but it was worth it.

I joined Adrian and told him to sit down on the couch.

I settled in next to him and started filling my plate with fried jalapeno poppers, onion rings, cheese, dip, and potato skins. "So these are all from your recipes," I said. "I picked out the ones I know you like the most that happen to go with some of my favorite memories."

I would've gone with his salsa too, if it weren't for the fact that the only memory I had of that evening was when Thea had projectile vomited over the table because she'd eaten too much.

"Yo, eat." I pointed to his empty plate.

"Right." He looked dazed. "I'm letting it sink in, you shit."

"Is it okay?" I got worried. "You should know I'm flyin' blind here. This was the best date I could come up with, and—"

"And it couldn't be better."

I breathed out in relief. "Thank fuck." Eyeing the table, I bit off a piece of bread and decided to go with the cherry tomatoes and sliced mozzarella first. "Okay, so the reason I went with that —" I gestured at the bowl "—was because you cut your finger when you were doing the tomatoes."

"Fond memory?" he drawled.

I nodded and swallowed what was in my mouth. "'Cause it was the first time I'd gotten fussy over someone other than Thea, and I liked it."

His gaze softened, and he grinned and shook his head. "Only you can turn me cutting myself into something sweet. Go on, I'm all ears."

If he thought that was sweet, hopefully he'd like the rest, too.

14

"You—you haven't eaten very much," I said, letting out a labored breath.

"Hmmm...as delicious as this was..." He sucked on my neck and trailed a hand down my chest to my crotch. "I can't focus on food anymore."

Shit, neither could I when he did that. A groan slipped past my lips when he squeezed my junk gently and rubbed it downward. It was time to find the courage to tell him what I'd practiced all morning to say.

After a lot of going back and forth, I'd decided...I was ready for more. More, in this case, was him fucking me. Adrian wanted it but had never once pressed the issue or even brought it up. Didn't mean I was blind or couldn't see where his fantasies went sometimes.

Physically, I'd been ready for a while. I'd jacked off thinking about it. I had no doubt he'd make it pleasurable for me. But somewhere along the road, I guessed I had created a mental block. It wasn't a trigger; I didn't fear anything or worry about pain. I just didn't wanna close myself off the way I'd automatically done so many times in the past. With Adrian, I wanted to enjoy it all.

"Fuck." I exhaled shakily as he unbuttoned my jeans and slipped a hand underneath my boxers. I thrust my hips slowly, grinding into his grip on me. "We should, um...put away the food. I don't want it to—fuck—go bad."

He groaned, fully aware I wouldn't let this go. I didn't waste anything.

"Come on." I pulled myself out of the haze and tucked my dick back into my pants. "It'll be quick."

"Cockblocker." He smirked ruefully.

I'd make it up to him in spades.

We carried the plates and all the food out to the kitchen, and Adrian being Adrian had to do it perfectly or not at all. So once we were there and the food was in the fridge, he filled the sink to do the dishes.

"Hey, we can do *that* tomorrow." I stood behind him and covered the bulge in his pants with my hand. Almost covered it. Okay, covered half of it.

"Perhaps I decided to punish you by not putting out," he said.

I grinned against his back and began unbuttoning his pants. "That's good, I guess." Turning him so he wasn't facing the sink, I dropped to my knees and pushed his pants down his hips. "It means I can put out instead." I glanced up at him as I wrapped my fingers around his cock.

His eyes were hooded. He stroked my cheek and whispered a curse as I leaned in and gave the head of his cock an open-mouthed kiss. "We don't have to rush anything," he murmured. "I haven't asked, but I know you have some..."

What, issues?

I chuckled and then sucked lightly on the head. "And I'm

thankful you're letting me work through them at my own pace, which is exactly what I'm doing. I want you to fuck me."

I grabbed his ass and pulled him down my throat before he could answer.

"Oh, *God*... Adrian—fuck!" I dug my head into the pillow and thrust deeper into his mouth. He sucked me deep and hard, and he was a merciless bastard. We'd been at it for over an hour, and at some point I was sure I'd gotten tears in my eyes 'cause I was so fucking desperate.

"I'm ready," I panted. "Mother of—" I gritted my teeth.

He made me wanna beg for his cock in my ass.

As it was, all I got was his mouth and two slick fingers teasing.

I shuddered violently, a sweaty mess. I no longer had the taste of him on my tongue.

My legs were spread. The invitation screamed *fuck me.*

"I'll hurt you," I growled.

Throwing an arm over my face, I moaned breathlessly and hated him as much as I lov—*fuuuck*. Not the time for another aha moment.

Adrian continued sucking my cock and fingering me slowly, and the fucking tears were back. I'd been close so many times. I deserved more. I needed to come, dammit. I needed his cock.

After I'd swallowed every drop in the kitchen, he'd hauled me into the bedroom and said he needed "a minute" to regroup. More like a thousand minutes, it felt like.

"Now," he breathed out.

I sucked air into my lungs, my heart slamming against my ribcage. I'd never been harder. My balls were full and tight, and the skin stretching around my dick was uncomfortable.

Kneeling in between my thighs, Teach coated his cock with lube and stroked himself sensually.

"Beg." The look in his eyes told me he wasn't taking any bullshit. I was about to get it, and I had to play nice.

"Please fuck me." I spoke in a rush. *Salivating.* I eye-fucked his cock. "I want it. Just you, nothing between us."

He bent forward, hovering over me, and whispered in my ear while he teased my ass with the tip of his wet, hard cock. "You have no clue how many times I've thought about this." His voice turned me into a feverish mess, and I couldn't tense up when he started pushing in slowly, even if I'd wanted to. "I've woken up to fading images of deep, sweaty fucking." He made me groan embarrassingly loud. "And all I've wanted to do was flip you over and fuck you so hard into next week that you've forgotten every name but mine."

Those images were assaulting me now, too. He went quiet and sank his teeth into my shoulder. The faintest moan puffed out in a breath when he was balls deep, and I needed to move. My hips rose, as if my ass had gotten greedy overnight.

I was a fucking puddle. He'd turned me on to the point where I was swimming in sex. Thoughts, taste, smell, touch— everything was sexual. Intimate. Hotter than hell.

"How the fuck do you do it," I breathed out, the question rhetorical. Or maybe not. I thought I'd get used to bottoming and enjoy it down the road—not this, where I couldn't wait to feel him. Then again, Adrian had been different from the get-go.

I moaned as he drove deep into me, and it dawned on me that he wasn't just my first kiss. He was my first everything. That was why shit was so different. They weren't related, what I'd done before and...this.

I became starved.

"Fuck me harder," I demanded, outta breath. "Oh, shit."

Adrian fucked me. He grabbed my jaw, kissed me passionately, and railed me like a man possessed. And I got off on it. I loved it. It fueled me, made me crave more—made me wanna let go of all inhibitions.

"Do you trust me?"

I nodded, trapped in the intensity of his gaze.

He nodded sharply and pulled out, the feeling causing me to wince.

"Get on all fours for me, Dominic."

That woke up my nerves. I'd be more vulnerable in that position, but I trusted him. I rolled over and pushed myself up, looking past my shoulder to see him.

"Close your eyes," he murmured. His hand slid down my spine. Warmly, slowly, soothingly. "Just feel."

I swallowed and complied. My head hung, and I closed my eyes.

He rubbed my ass cheeks, taking his time, and teased my now semihard cock with the tips of his fingers. I shivered in return. Then he shifted closer, the head of his cock entering me. After that, it was slower than slowest. I clenched involuntarily. He shuddered, setting off one for me, too. Oh God, it was amazing.

Every inch he gave me rubbed the best places, and it was slow enough for me to savor each sensation. I learned where I was sensitive. I discovered a part of me that was superfocused and could zoom in on whatever he did. My heart rate spiked, yet my mind calmed down.

On one long stroke, he brushed past something that made me choke on a gasp. His laugh was low, sexy as sin, and he gripped my hips tightly. He fucked that spot. Never breaking the pace, never faltering.

Pressure built in my gut. I was almost dizzy. I heard myself mumbling, panting, asking for more.

"Come here." He sat back on his heels and pulled me with

him. Those warm hands of his went up and down my torso. "Fuck yourself on my cock. Make it yours."

I groaned and lolled my head along his shoulder. "It already fucking is. Or I'll be pissed."

Unbidden, I thought how everything could've played out differently. Me turning him down out of fear. Us being friends. I'd be his homeless buddy who slept in his car, and he'd meet someone. He'd live his life without me.

"Hell no," I grunted under my breath. That was sickening.

"What?" He fisted my dick and stroked it firmly, his own breathing labored and hot against my neck.

"Nothing. Oh, yeah..." I sank down on him. "Incredible."

"A bit too incredible," he groaned. "I'm almost there."

"Mmm..." I tilted my face and licked his neck. Salty, fresh, masculine. I was pretty fucking useless at this point, so he took over. "You gonna fill me up and claim my ass?" I laughed, bordering on delirious.

The pleasure was incomprehensible and all-consuming. I moved fluidly and followed his commands. His cock stretched me, causing my own dick to leak. The smell was... My mouth watered.

"That's already mine, darling," he whispered gravelly. "You, my crass, sweet, amazing man, are all mine."

"Yeah." I grinned like a fool, though a couple seconds later, the fog of the high wore off. My senses sharpened, and it was all about the chase. Adrian pushed me forward again, and I gripped the headboard as he fucked me into oblivion.

My lungs burned, reminding me I needed to breathe.

The sound that escaped me as he tightened his grip on my cock was more of a sob than anything else.

"*Fuck!*" Adrian let out a strained growl. Next, he came at me from a different angle that made my eyes flash open.

"Oh shit, oh God," I gasped.

My knees shook, every muscle in me protested, and then I was fucking flying. A drawn-out moan left my throat as I started coming. Adrian fucked me faster. All I heard was skin slapping. All I felt was pure bliss. All I smelled was intimacy.

He rocked into me once more and came with a low hiss.

Months ago, the idea of this kind of fucking would've given me nightmares. Actually, it would've shut off my emotions. I would've merely taken it. But now...now, I could look forward to next time. And there would be a next time. Adrian fucked like a god.

"Don't ever—make me choose...between sex and food," I panted, collapsing on the mattress. I grimaced at the mess I'd landed in. "Can't...move..."

Adrian rolled me over onto my back, his muscular arms caging me in, and he kissed me hotly. We were both completely out of breath, and how he could go on, I had no idea.

"That was the sexiest..." He drew in a breath through his nose and nuzzled my jaw. "Fuckin'..." Dipping down, he kissed my chest, teased my nipples with his teeth, and then swiped the tip of his tongue over the wet spot across my abs.

"Shit, stop!" I tensed up and laughed.

"Why?" He did it again.

I glared, though it was difficult to stop laughing. "Because it fucking tickles."

He grinned and cupped my cheek, kissing me softly then deeply.

"The sheets are nasty," I mumbled against his mouth. I licked his bottom lip, tasting my come. "Let's shower."

It was as if Adrian couldn't stop smiling in the shower. He

couldn't stop kissing me either, and I had *no* complaints about that.

"You're acting like a lovesick fool," I chuckled.

He laughed under his breath, head bowed as I massaged shampoo into his hair. "Maybe I am."

That put a lump in my throat. "Me, too."

What he saw in me, I wasn't sure I'd ever understand.

What I saw in him...? The list was endless.

Adrian lifted his head and searched my eyes.

"I mean it." I nodded. "It's difficult to explain, but you're my home. I'll do my best to never lose it."

He sighed with relief and pulled me under the spray, his hug almost as warm as the water. "Let's not lose each other, then." He tilted his head and covered my mouth with his. I stroked his back, feeling his muscles flexing as he held me tighter. "You and Thea are my home, too."

And he wanted to discuss vacations? Christ. How could he not see this—all this—was a vacation?

"You're absolutely sure it's not too much?" I asked once more. "I won't get over my hang-ups tomorrow."

"It'd be weird if you did." He kissed me once more and then began soaping up my body in slow, sensual strokes. "You're very focused on money, how much you feel you owe, what things are worth, et cetera. That will take time, and I have all the patience in the world, I promise."

Good. I'd need a lot of reminders.

"As for Thea..." He lifted a brow, gaze trained on my arm. "For the sake of...everything, I suppose, consider the fact that I love her wholeheartedly. I adore that girl. What if—what if I wished she were mine, as well?"

My mouth was suddenly dry. "Do you?"

"Very much." He looked me in the eye at that.

"Oh."

What the fuck did I say to that? Here, have half my daughter? That was weird as fuck. However, the thought of us being a family made me wanna cry like a bitch. In a good way. It was overwhelming and unbelievable, yet Adrian made it possible. And because of him, just him, I wanted it.

"Yeah." I nodded jerkily, getting mushy, so it was all I could say. "I can't—um, talk."

He let out a soft, breathy laugh and shook his head. "Neither can I."

I could tell, so I kissed him instead, my mind alternating between being completely blank and full of things I wanted to say. Mostly, it was shit I wanted to thank him for. Promises I wanted to make. Then again, it was better I made them to myself. He'd see. I'd show him.

I'd also do my damnedest not to act like I was a burden. For whatever reasons, he'd chosen me and Thea. He saw good in us —and potential, I hoped.

"Billy's gonna be a smug prick when we see him," I said with a groan. "He's always been telling me 'One day, kid. One day you'll find the luck. One day you'll see what life is really about.' Fucker."

"You mean you have to admit defeat because he was right?"

"Yeah."

"You poor bastard," he deadpanned.

"That's what I'm sayin'."

He fought a smirk and pinched my ass, and I snickered.

15

In the days leading up to our trip to Florida, I had focused solely on Thea's comfort. Changes scared her sometimes, so I'd only thought about making it comfortable and painless for her. Adrian and I had managed to borrow a car seat for her, we'd bought her favorite snacks, a coloring book, and Willow had stopped by with headphones for her.

Turned out, Thea was just fine. She stiffened and was anxious the minute we reached the airport in Seattle, but she relaxed once we got through security. I held her the entire time, and by the time we boarded the plane, she was even a little excited. Anxious and nervous, but excited.

Adrian had told her stories about flying. She'd found them funny.

I had not.

I should've considered what flying for the first time would do to *me*.

Thea wanted the window seat so she could look out. I ended up in the middle, and I clutched the armrests for all I was worth.

"Are you all right?" Adrian frowned as he buckled his seatbelt.

I jerked a nod.

The plane was nearly full, and flight attendants came out to do some demonstration on safety and how to handle shit if we were crashing. At the same time, the plane moved and began taxiing out.

I looked up to see where a mask would drop down in case we were about to die.

"You know, people really don't fucking belong in the air," I said tightly. "There's *nothing* wrong with taking the goddamn bus."

"Hey." Adrian grabbed my hand firmly, his eyes flashing with concern. But there was something else, too. He lowered his voice. "Maybe you don't say that with young ears listening?"

"Right." Shit.

His mouth twitched. "Okay. Anything I can do?" He rubbed soothing circles along my hand.

I didn't see that soothing working if we crashed.

"Is it too late to take the bus?" I asked.

"Afraid so."

Fuck this day. As if this wasn't enough, there'd be a second flight, too. We had a connection in Atlanta.

When the lights went out in the cabin, I almost panicked. "What's going on? Why the fuck did the lights—"

"Easy, baby," he whispered. "It's protocol. When you fly at night, they turn down the lights."

"Oh." I swallowed and went even more rigid as we picked up more speed. "Holy shit."

My knuckles were white.

Next thing I knew, we were airborne and going up, up, up, up.

Adrian squeezed my hand hard. "I love you."

"Oh, fuck you," I forced out. We were going to crash. This couldn't be normal. We were turning, and the entire fucking plane might as well have tipped the fuck over. "You're telling me that now? This is the motherfucking moment you pick to spell it out?"

The plane finally leveled out, and I indulged in a long breath.

"Jesus," I said shakily. I turned to Adrian, a bit nauseated, but this couldn't wait. "I love you, too. And I might pick up drinking."

He laughed and brought our clasped hands to his lips. "While we're at it, perhaps cleaning up your language—"

"Not the time," I told him. "If we survive this, we can discuss it."

"Noted." He was doing a shitty job of hiding his amusement. Which was at my expense. Prick. "How are you feeling now?"

"Like we should've taken the bus."

It was a long night, and the second flight from Atlanta to Jacksonville wasn't much easier than the first. Thea slept through most of it. Adrian had managed to doze on and off.

I'd been so tense the entire time that when we landed in Jacksonville, I was exhausted and sore all over.

Easter arrived pretty late this year, so it was already warm in Florida.

It was cool seeing palm trees.

I grabbed our bags while Adrian carried Thea, and rather than taking a cab, he'd suggested we rent a car. He'd looked up Jacksonville and told me it was a large city, and being able to drive wherever was the best option.

Half an hour later, he was behind the wheel and taking us away from the airport.

He asked if I could punch the address to Billy's brother's house into the GPS. I gave him a funny look, and he did it himself.

Like I knew that shit?

With the flights from hell behind me, the adrenaline rush was settling. We were here to see Billy. He was dying. It wasn't one of those vacations Adrian had mentioned. I was here to say goodbye to the man who'd been more like a dad to me than anyone else.

I almost asked Thea if she remembered Billy, but I doubted that. By now, Willow, Adrian, and I were in agreement that Thea's memory was outta this world. Not really eidetic, but close. That said, she'd only been a year old the one and only time I'd brought her to visit Billy. I'd been staying with him a lot 'cause Aunt Chrissy's boyfriend had been another class-act douchebag.

Billy's brother lived in a small neighborhood near the beach, the streets lined with everything from fancy beach houses to renovated shacks. At the end of one street, the GPS declared we had arrived at our destination.

"I don't even want to know what property costs here." Adrian glanced out the window and killed the engine. "Nice house." He slid on his shades and stepped out.

I looked at said house, stalling. It wasn't over the top, but yeah, it was very nice. One story, wood framing, painted light green, white shutters. Pine trees shot up behind the house. There were no cars in the driveway.

When Adrian had taken Thea, I let out a breath, sucked it up, and left the car, too.

Billy stepped out of the house, effectively turning me into a kid again. He wasn't leaning on his cane any heavier than usual, but he had changed a bit. He'd lost some weight, and he looked frailer.

"Go, baby." Adrian nodded at the house. "I've got this."

I hesitated, wanting to hide behind Thea, before I managed to get my legs to work. I wouldn't be able to front with Billy. I'd crack in a fucking minute.

"You stubborn shit," he said with a lazy smirk.

"I guess." I climbed up the steps leading to the narrow porch. "Hey."

"Hey, kid." He waved me closer. "Don't just stand there. Give a dying man a hug."

"You asshole," I whispered. My eyes welled up as I closed the last distance, and then I was hugging Billy for the first time.

His hugs were as firm as his handshakes. Give him cancer, give him a cane. He was still military to the bone.

"I'm glad you're stubborn," he whispered back thickly.

I screwed my eyes shut and inhaled shakily. He smelled the same. Smoke and Old Spice. It was familiar.

He'd smacked me upside the head one time when I'd stolen him a gift set of Old Spice for his birthday. I hadn't fucking known what to get people, and I'd seen that in a store, remembering his body wash.

He'd smiled, too. And shaken his head at me.

"Come on, lemme meet your family. Then we eat." Billy clapped my back before ending the hug. "My sister-in-law cooked up a storm before they left."

"Where are they?" I asked. Looking back toward the car, I waved Adrian over and wiped my cheek with the back of my hand.

"They decided to give us privacy, so they took the girls down to Orlando," Billy replied. He squinted down the path to the street. "I thought you said he was a teacher."

"He is."

Billy huffed. "In my day, teachers didn't look like tattoo artists."

"In your day?" I cocked a brow. "You're like fifty." Then I shook my head. It didn't matter. Adrian climbed the porch steps with Thea, a polite smile on his handsome face. "This is Billy. Billy—Adrian, Thea."

"Good to meet you, Adrian." Billy extended his hand. "Dominic's told me a lot about you."

"Likewise, and it's an honor." Adrian shook it firmly, then kissed Thea's cheek. She was hiding, shy. "Can you wave hello to Billy, princess?"

I grinned, 'cause my man was hot as fuck when he got all Daddylike.

She burrowed closer against Adrian's neck, so she wasn't ready.

Billy smiled. "There's no rush. Let's head out back. I gotta sit my old ass down."

He did look worn and tired.

On the way through the house, he showed us our guest room and informed us, with a smirk, that we were lucky his brother wasn't home. If he had been, he would've insisted Adrian and I sleep in separate bedrooms because we weren't married.

"I would've lied and said we got hitched last week," I replied with a shrug.

I dumped our shit on the bed, and then Billy asked if I could raid the fridge for something to eat. He was a bit outta breath. I could tell he needed to sit down stat, so I agreed, and Adrian followed Billy outside.

Reaching the fridge, I raised my brows upon opening the door. Billy was right. His sister-in-law had cooked a shitload for him, presumably so he wouldn't have to do much. That made me happy. It was about time someone took care of him the way he deserved.

I found a tray and filled it with lemonade, sandwiches, pickles, and yogurt. Thea liked that brand, I knew. After adding some plates, a spoon for the yogurt, and napkins, I headed outside.

The back porch was big, half of it in the shade. The trees shielded us from most of the sun, but not the pool. It shone bright blue, and Thea couldn't take her eyes off it.

"This okay?" I set the tray on the table.

"Perfect," Billy grunted as he sat forward and snatched up a sandwich. "If you don't have a swimsuit for Thea, my youngest niece ain't much older than her. There should be somethin' in her room that fits."

"That would be cool." I was more sleepy than hungry, so I only poured a glass of lemonade for now. "How're you doin'?"

Billy paused, sandwich midair. "I'm good. Constantly tired. Got good painkillers, though."

Adrian shifted Thea on his lap and gave her the yogurt. "If there's anything we can do..."

"I appreciate it." Billy nodded and dug into his food. "Now, eat. Your girl's skin and bones. Don't'chu have food in Washington?"

"Picky eater." I poked Thea's tummy, and she scowled and grinned at the same time. "She eats more now though, since Adrian's cooking."

"One taste of fried gator and she won't wanna leave Florida," Billy promised.

I grimaced. That sounded fucking nasty.

"It's good, actually." Adrian was amused by my expression.

"I'll take your word for it." I smirked sarcastically and reached for the pickles.

Adrian and Billy eased into a conversation about Florida. I'd forgotten that Adrian's parents had retired and lived here now, though they were down in the south.

I bit off a piece of pickle and glanced around me. We were staying here four days, and while Billy's condition made me feel shitty about calling it a vacation, I guessed it would be in some ways. My first one.

The pool did look inviting. I'd never been in one before.

On the way here, I'd seen locals wearing jackets. Crazy fuckers. It was the hottest spring as far as I was concerned.

"He tried to mug me," I heard Billy chuckle gruffly.

My head whipped around, and he explained that Adrian had asked how Billy and I met.

"What the fuck?" I glared. "Why you gotta scare him away?"

Adrian found that funny. "How innocent do you think I am, Dominic? More importantly, how innocent do you think I believe *you* are?"

"I don't know, but there's no need for reminders." I angrily bit off another piece of pickle. "I've done shit, end of. I ain't proud, but I'm not ashamed either. It's just..." I shrugged. "Whatever."

"You shouldn't be ashamed." Adrian wiped his hands, finished with his sandwich. He didn't look bothered at all. "I'm under no illusions. You did what you could to survive and provide for Thea. Am I thrilled that some resort to crime and hurting others? Of course not, but *why* they have to resort to crime is a more important issue."

"Told you he was a teacher," I muttered to Billy with a wry smile. "He likes to lecture."

"Keep him," was all Billy said.

"I'm trying!" I wagged the pickle at him, frustrated. "But you gotta bring up that I tried to mug you."

They just laughed at me.

"To be fair, I asked." Adrian leaned over and kissed my cheek.

Yeah, yeah.

"Want me to take her?" I nodded at Thea. At his bitch look, I held up my palms. "Yo, I only asked 'cause you've haven't had a break in a while. That's me being *polite* and shit."

"Oh." He loosened up. "Well, I have three years to catch up on. I'll let you know if I need a break."

Billy waved a finger between us. "You sound like an old married couple. I like it."

After a day of catching up and chilling, I slept like a log until Adrian woke me up at the ass-crack of dawn the following morning.

He wanted to see the sunrise.

"Gimme a minute," I grumbled.

Thea was dressed and ready to go, and when I emerged from our room, I saw Billy was up, too. They'd packed breakfast for us and had the whole fucking day planned out.

"How long have you been up?" I yawned and side-eyed Adrian.

"A while."

Despite that the beach was only a couple minutes down the road, we took the car so Billy wouldn't exhaust himself before the day had even begun. Blankets, towels, food, one excited three-year-old in a purple bathing suit and a fucking tutu, and we were off.

The parking lot at the beach was deserted, no fucking

surprise there, though Billy said there could be a crowd in the mornings. The weather was supposed to be hot and sunny today too, so we wouldn't be alone for long.

"Do you need help?" I asked Billy as we reached the sand.

He waved that off, too damn proud.

Adrian set up a beach chair for Billy, fanned out a blanket, and set an umbrella in the sand for later when the sun was up, all while I struggled to put sunblock on a kid who only had eyes for the ocean.

The horizon burned red, moments away from being lit up for the day.

It was peaceful.

"It's not that warm, hon," I told Thea as she went to remove her ridiculous skirt. "Wait 'til after breakfast."

She pouted. Then scowled when I put on her cotton cardigan again.

"I'm not hungry," she signed.

"Come on, princess." Adrian stood up and held out his hand. "We can see if there are some pretty shells to bring home."

She was on board with that, and the two trailed hand in hand down to the water.

Still sleepy, I sat back on the blanket next to Billy's chair. I pulled up my legs a bit and rested my forearms on them.

Billy sighed contentedly and sparked up a smoke. "It's gonna be a good day."

"You gonna let me bum one?" I held out two fingers.

He tossed me the pack. "Don't I always?"

I grinned. "I'm your favorite moocher, don't deny it."

He huffed a laugh. "I'd use many words for you, Dominic. Moocher ain't one."

Taking a drag from my smoke, I peered out over the beach. Aside from someone walking their dog farther away, I only saw Adrian and Thea running after each other by the water.

She kicked water his way, to which he crouched down before pretending to pounce. Peals of laughter and squeals rang out from Thea, and I smiled like a fucking schmuck.

Maybe I wasn't a moocher, generally speaking. I'd had a lot of help, regardless. Without Billy and Adrian, I couldn't even imagine where I'd be today. It scared the ever-loving shit outta me to consider it.

"I wanna do what you've done, Billy." I blew out some smoke and rested my chin on my knee. "I think it's the only way I'll find balance. If I can help someone the way you've helped me..."

"Well. You've got a good thing goin' on down at that place —the Quad?"

"Yeah." I watched as Thea picked up a shell and placed it in Adrian's palm for safekeeping. "Yeah, I like it there. Adrian's awesome with kids. Everyone listens to him."

Billy hummed. "They'll listen to you, too. I reckon you'll make a perfect team."

"How so?" I was almost too chickenshit to face him.

"Don't you see it?" He smiled faintly and leaned forward in his seat. "You both have your vulnerabilities, strengths, weaknesses, and big hearts. You're crude and street where he's eloquent and well-read, but it works when you want the exact same fuckin' thing. And he's real. I like that." He nodded, and I took a final drag from my smoke before sticking it down in the sand. "He's not some pompous suit who went to college and only believed what he read in books."

That was true. From an early point, he'd become a part of communities where they tried to help.

Billy squeezed my shoulder. "Stick together, son. You'll see. You're good for each other."

I swallowed hard, absently tilting my head to lean my cheek on his hand that remained on my shoulder. Adrian and Thea stood together, watching the sun rise. Feet sinking into the wet sand.

Minutes ticked by. The sun rose higher, and something solidified inside me. I believed in Adrian and me. Billy was right. We could be very good together, if we weren't already. I guessed I would have doubts about myself for some time, but I'd never been a quitter. I wasn't gonna start.

I'd show everyone—most of all, myself.

"Have you told him you love him yet?" Billy asked.

I would've chuckled if the melancholy wasn't so damn heavy. "Yeah. He did, too."

"Good. That makes me happy." He gave my shoulder another squeeze, then leaned back in his seat.

I blew out a breath. I needed some sense of relief. I knew that made me greedy, given how much I had now. "You know what fucking sucks?" I glanced back at him. "I get the first taste of what it's like to have a real family, and then we lose you."

For once in my life, my heart was brimming. I felt so much. I was *happy*. I was in love, and I had my daughter. She was safe. A happy kid. We had food on the table. We had a home with Adrian, a man who wanted both of us. Called us his.

There was a bright future that I wanted to share with the limping grunt next to me.

He nodded, glistening eyes on the horizon. "Yeah, it hurts like a bitch." He was blunt. I'd always liked that about him. No bullshit. "I've made my peace with it, though. This is life, and knowing you, you'll make it a lesson. You ain't one to live in the past, Dominic. And I guess—"

"If you deliver some poetic crap about not appreciating the sunshine without a little rain here and there, I swear to Christ, I'll hurt you."

He laughed gruffly. "Fair enough. Nothing poetic."

Good.

The sun wasn't touching the horizon anymore, and Thea had gone back to collecting shells. Adrian, on the other hand, looked ready to come back here and maybe have breakfast.

Thinking ahead, I reached for the bag we'd brought. Coffee, OJ, leftover sandwiches, and pancakes made for one hell of a breakfast on the beach. At fuck-no o'clock in the morning.

"I'm really glad you came, Dominic." Billy accepted a cup of coffee with a nod. "It means a lot, getting to meet Adrian and Thea. Seeing you happy."

I had no time to reply before Adrian and Thea raced back to us, our girl fist-pumping the air 'cause she won. But I thought a lot about what Billy had said while we ate. Thea snuggled up in my lap, wrapped in a fluffy towel, and I decided to give Billy what he wanted. A few days of proper family time, the way I saw us in my mind.

I'd be a miserable motherfucker when I lost him, so I'd be stupid to start mourning now. I had too little time. What I had, I wanted to fill with memories I could keep forever.

"I'm surprised you haven't asked for ketchup yet," Billy noted. "You used to put that nasty shit on everything."

I laughed. "I live with a chef. Firstly, he'd cut off my hand if I asked for ketchup—"

"I really would." Adrian winked.

"And secondly, I don't need it anymore." I lifted one shoulder and took a big bite of my sandwich. "That doesn't mean I don't sometimes steal condiments at Diego's place, though. He has these little packets for those who order to-go. Free is free."

"*That's* why I keep finding salt and pepper from his place at the bottom of the laundry basket." Adrian looked like he'd just solved the biggest math problem. It was funny. "I assumed you were handing those out to customers and forgot they were in your pockets."

I smirked. "So you *do* think I'm innocent."

"I was clearly wrong." He pretended to be disappointed. "I can understand muggings and almost anything else, but having sticky fingers for condiments is a hard pill to swallow."

I leaned over and gave him a smooch, accidentally getting some mayo on the corner of his mouth. "You're stuck with me. Sorry."

"I suppose I'll live." He smiled that lazy smile as I wiped away the mayo with my thumb.

Thea grunted and pushed me back, evidently not pleased her personal chair was moving.

"You three are sickeningly cute." Billy shook his head at us, mirth in his eyes. "Now that I know you're in it for the long haul, I reserve the right to change tactics and tease Dominic for becoming whipped."

I almost ruined the moment by telling him he could say whatever he wanted, as long as it made him happy.

Instead, I widened my arms and gave him my cockiest expression. "Bring it, ya old fool."

Something told me I was about to have one of the best weeks of my life. One where I was also constantly on the verge of tears.

EPILOGUE

A FEW YEARS DOWN THE ROAD

"Are you sure you don't want to stay a while longer?" Adrian asked as he pulled over in the parking lot. "We're happy to have you, you know that."

I shook my head. "You've done so much already."

He sighed and stepped outside. "Figured you might say that. I'll be back in five."

Closing the door, he left me in the backseat with Thea while he went inside the Quad to get Dominic.

They were preparing for a crapload that would happen this weekend. Fund raiser, coat drive, soup kitchen—whatever. The church was involved too, and the committee Dominic was in charge of had named the event "All For All." There would be a massive version of a garage sale, all proceeds going to the Quad for new computers, self-defense classes, bus passes, food, workshops, and clothes. Whatever was necessary.

Dominic was a persuasive dude, so he'd gotten free advertising in the paper. They were expecting a big crowd, and I hoped it went well. He and Adrian had worked their asses off.

It was cool that some of the kids would end up with jobs, too —fingers crossed. A list had been put up on the bulletin board inside the Quad, and for weeks, we'd been able to put down things like babysitting, lawn mowing, cleaning, dog walking, and so on. Plus recommended rates.

I wouldn't be here for that.

I'd finally graduated from high school. I was free. As of last week, I was also eighteen.

Adrian and Dominic had kindly taken me in, and I'd stayed on their couch the past couple of months. I'd tried to stick it out at home, but I hadn't been able to take another of Dad's beatings.

Thea slid me a note that said "I'm going to miss you."

I managed a wobbly grin. "Me too. We'll email each other, though." I gave her pinkie a little squeeze. "Why don't you use the tablet?"

It was what she communicated with in school. One of those fancy, special schools up in Ponderosa. They'd each been given a tablet with various apps for communicating through electronic voices.

She scrunched her nose and wrote another note. "I sound like a silly robot!"

I chuckled. Maybe it did sound silly, but she was still the cutest and smartest nine-year-old I'd ever met. Dimples, curly hair, two left feet, and all.

Adrian headed back to the car, this time with a scowling Dominic in tow.

They got in the front, and Dominic glanced back at me, frowning.

"Look, I don't see why you gotta fucking leave yet. Where's the goddamn fire?"

"Sweetheart." There was a hint of warning in Adrian's tone. He placed his hand on Dominic's thigh, then cocked a brow at me in the rearview. "But he does have a point."

I smirked and rolled my eyes, facing the window instead. They knew very well why I was leaving.

———

Leaning my head against the window, I watched the trees whoosh by in a blur of green. Washington was all I knew, and it'd be exciting to discover what California had to offer.

My grandma waited for me there. I'd live with her, which I had never considered to be a possibility until Adrian had intervened and convinced me to tell her about my home situation. She'd had no idea her son was a prick, and I'd cried like a pussy —from sheer relief—when she'd instantly taken my side. More than that, she believed me.

I'd come back to visit, though.

Adrian, Dominic, and Thea had given me my first glimpse of what a true family was. It was because of them I felt so motivated to start over somewhere else. I wanted what they shared in their modest, cozy two-bedroom apartment by Olympia Square.

I wanted the photos they had on the walls. Beaches, goofy grins, hugs, kisses, birthday celebrations, snowcapped mountains, sunburns, and funny faces. During the time I stayed with them, I'd memorized three photos that fueled me. Proof that this kind of love existed. Thea was in the first one. A look of concentration on her face as she blew out eight candles on a chocolate cake. She was wearing a T-shirt in the picture that said "Daddy's girl x 2, so don't mess with me."

When I turned eight, my grandma sent a card with fifty dollars that my dad gambled away.

My second favorite photo was of Adrian and Dominic squatting down with Thea in between them. There were palm trees in the background, and their noses and cheeks were red from the sun. They'd gone to Hawaii one summer, though their wide smiles weren't reserved for vacations. I'd seen them plenty.

My dad had taken me to Reno once. There were vague memories of cigarette smoke, the annoying ding of slot machines, and him smacking me around when he'd lost too much money.

Last but not least, probably my absolute favorite photo. Taken in a restaurant in Jacksonville a few years ago, it showed Dominic, Adrian, Thea, and a man named Billy. Dominic referred to the old man as his pop these days, though I knew that hadn't always been the case. Billy had passed away from cancer shortly after that trip, so Dominic probably cherished that memory for other reasons.

For me, seeing that picture and hearing the stories behind it, I had learned family came in all sizes and forms. It wasn't merely a mom, dad, kid, and grandparent. They weren't all related by blood. But it worked, and I wanted that more than anything.

Thanks to Adrian and Dominic, I would have extended family up here and a reason to visit. Thanks to them, I didn't only have awful memories of our town.

It was bittersweet, arriving at the Greyhound station in Seattle.

There were people everywhere.

I had my ticket, my bag, and the container of food Adrian had packed for me.

"Now I know what Billy felt when I left Philly," Dominic muttered, to which Adrian kissed their linked hands. "Kid, I'm warning you—" He pointed at me. "If you don't call, I'mma come down there to California and tear your punk ass a new one."

"I'll call," I promised, grinning nervously. This was it. I was excited and terrified at the same time. "Hey...thank you." I swallowed. "I don't know what I would've done without you."

Adrian stepped forward and hugged me tightly. "Don't be a stranger, okay? You can come up whenever you want."

I nodded, trusting him. Them. From the moment they took me in and said they'd be with me every step of the way, they'd shown me not all grown-ups were like my dad.

Dominic hugged me too—and threw in a couple more threats for good measure—and Thea and I bumped fists. Then she informed me my bus had Wi-Fi, so I better not make her wait long for her email.

"I wouldn't dare keep you waiting, Thea." I smirked and kissed the top of her head.

"You got money?" Dominic asked.

I threw Adrian a look. "Yeah, 'cause your man fucking forced me to accept it."

He'd given me forty bucks and sworn he'd call my grandmother to say I'd missed my bus if I didn't take it.

When I told Dominic this, he laughed and said he loved it when Adrian played dirty.

Then they announced over the PA system that my bus was about to board, and it kinda killed the mood.

"Goddammit." Dominic blew out a breath.

The guys hugged me once more, and I hiked up my bag. My throat closed up, so I couldn't speak. Thankfully, they understood and appeared to be on the same page.

This is it.

I nodded sharply, then turned around to get on the bus.

I was ready to find my own home.

I knew what it was supposed to be like now.

CARA DEE

Excerpt from *When Forever Ended*, the second Camassia Cove novel

I released a breath and tried to collect myself, failing miserably. The note landed on the desk, and I covered my face with my hands. Never before had I felt so fucking weak and pathetic. There was no fight in me. I cried at nothing. Or I was careless and stoic. Or I was riddled with guilt and anxiety.

Self-control used to be important to me. Now I didn't have an ounce of it left, and it was tearing me apart.

It's been a month. You said once a month was okay.

It *wasn't* okay. I just couldn't resist for longer than a month.

Unlocking the drawer, I blinked away the tears and stared at the stack of photos I kept hidden. Childhood memories. I fanned them out and saw the grin I was sporting in most pictures. I was Brady's age there. Pale in the beginning of summer, tan at the end. Camps, bonfires, beach fun, stealing Dad's boat...

Kelly.

Where I was, he was. His grins were cocky and full of attitude. A reckless kid. I was calm where he was wild. Born on the same day.

"Hey, happy birthday, idiot." He leaned against the locker next to mine and smirked.

"You too, dick." I shut my locker, turning to him. "Why do you look like you've just done something stupid I'll have to bail you out for later?"

"Oh, that's hurtful!" He clutched his heart, only to snort and throw an arm around my shoulders. "I don't think my best friend should be so cruel to me."

I tried not to smile. "Some best friend, eh?"

He nodded. "The worst. But at least he promised me forever." He took off down the hall before I could whack him with my history book.

"We said that when we were ten, jackass!" I hollered after him.

"Still counts!" His laughter echoed as he disappeared around the corner. "Forever, Will! Forever my bitch!"

I crumpled and wiped my cheek with the back of my hand. Twenty-four years since he left, and I still missed him so much it hurt. If only I could take back what I did.

One of my favorites was the photo his mother took of us on graduation day. Kelly had lost his cap; I was holding mine. We wore the same stupid smiles, equally excited about summer.

It was supposed to be the best one yet, until I fucked it all up.

"I thought you were my friend!" he shouted angrily. I reeled back in horror. I'd never seen him look so disgusted. I swallowed hard while he wiped his mouth and gave me a death glare. *"You fucking kissed me, you sick freak!"*

I flinched. My fingers shook as I piled the photos together, tucked them away, and promptly slammed the drawer shut. It'd be another month before I went there again.

Breathe.

I'm sorry, I'm sorry, I'm sorry.

I clutched my stomach and shut my eyes, and I rode out the waves of grief and shame that ultimately blurred the memories. Grins faded, dreams evaporated, fantasies were doused in gasoline and set on fire, and the past was buried once more.

MORE FROM CARA DEE

In Camassia Cove, everyone has a story to share

Cash
Willow
Lola
Justin

Though each Camassia Cove novel is a standalone within the series, the characters tend to make appearances in other titles. Cara freely admits she's addicted to revisiting the men and women who yammer in her head. If you enjoyed *Home*, you might like the following.

When Forever Ended
Uncomplicated Choices
Out

Check out Cara's collection at www.caradeewrites.com, and

don't forget to sign up for her newsletter so you don't miss any new releases, updates on book signings, giveaways, and much more.

ABOUT CARA

I'm often stoically silent or, if the topic interests me, a chronic rambler. In other words, I can discuss writing forever and ever.

Fiction, in particular. The love story—while a huge draw and constantly present—is secondary for me, because there's so much more to writing romance fiction than just making two (or more) people fall in love and have hot sex. There's a world to build, characters to develop, interests to create, and a topic or two to research thoroughly.

Every book is a challenge for me, an opportunity to learn something new, and a puzzle to piece together. I want my characters to come to life, and the only way I know to do that is to give them substance—passions, history, goals, quirks, and strong opinions—and to let them evolve.

Additionally, I want my men and women to be relatable. That means allowing room for everyday problems and, for lack of a better word, flaws. My characters will never be perfect.

Wait...this was supposed to be about me, not my writing.

I'm a writey person who loves to write. Always wanderlusting, twitterpating, kinking, and geeking. There's time for hockey and cupcakes, too. But mostly, I just love to write.

~CARA.

Made in the USA
Monee, IL
18 November 2019